TRUE WOMEN
Cookbook

by

Janice Woods Windle

erect dayflower

Texas bindweed

violet

Texas bluebonnets

purple
prairie clover

pointed phlox

rel

Indian blanket

spider lily

phlox

Texas bluebonnets

foxglove

meadow pink

Texas bluebonnets

-the-
ntain

Indian blanket

devil's claw

DORY GRACE '96

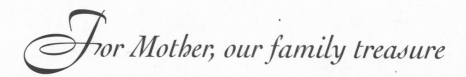

For Mother, our family treasure

Front cover portrait of Little Virginia King and back cover portrait of Sarah McClure Braches were painted by artist Anne Bell. Drawings of historic homes were drawn by artist Nacho Garcia.

Published by Bright Books, 2313 Lake Austin Boulevard, Austin, Texas 78703 (512) 499-4164

Printed in the United States of America
10 9 8 7 6 5 4 3 2 1

ISBN 1-880092-41-7

BRIGHT
BOOKS

Contents

It was Mother
who first told me
the stories of
True Women.

The Recipe
for True Women

This is the story of a family cookbook that grew into a best-selling novel, and then a CBS mini-series. The story began about ten years ago, at my mother's home in Seguin, Texas. It was a year or so after my father's death, and some weeks after I had lost a dear aunt as well; meanwhile, my older son was working on plans for a June wedding. I had been doing a lot of thinking about the past and the future, generations and regeneration, home and family.

I had come for a weekend visit, intending to spend a night in Seguin before flying home to El Paso the next day. But that night it began to snow and sleet. So my mother did not take me to the airport. Instead, I spent another night in the old family homeplace, and before I knew it, I had begun writing *True Women*.

That winter day, as we were talking at my mother's dining room table, the idea came to me for a very special wedding gift for my son Wayne and his bride, Mary Jane—something that would be more personal than anything they would ever see in a store. I decided to collect the favorite recipes from my mother, my aunts, and my cousins—and put together a family cookbook. Warming to my theme, I told my mother that it would become an heirloom, to be passed on to their children and even to their grandchildren. "If it's going to be handed down in the family," my mother said, getting up to dig in a kitchen drawer, "you should look at these recipes that belonged to my grandmother Bettie, and Aunt Annie, and Euphemia Texas Ashby King." Soon I was holding a scrapbook of hand-written recipes more than a century old.

Of course, I had heard about Euphemia and Bettie and the others many times. Stories about the women in the family had been passed down mother to daughter, grandmother to granddaughter, aunt to niece, and yes, even from father to daughter, for five generations. But when I had tried before to retell the vivid stories to my own children, who had grown up in a big city far from the small towns where those women had lived, these skeptical young citizens of the next generation had challenged me —"*Is that true? Are these women real?*" So to be sure that the epic tales honoring the women in the family would be passed along with the recipes, I knew I would need to include convincing evidence, with dates and details of historical events and some realistic descriptions of the places. And I would need to tie the stories together in a way that would make sense.

I asked my mother, Virginia Bergfeld Woods, to help me write up a few pages about each woman to go with the recipes. She is a well-respected historian who has served as a Trustee of the Alamo. Her shelves are lined with books about Texas history, and under her bed she stores boxes of genealogical research material. To my mother, the subjects have always been completely intertwined. And so to help with the answer to my questions, she spread a roll of white shelf paper across the dining room table and made a time-line of events in Texas history, marking off the lives of Euphemia, Aunt Annie, and Bettie. With their recipes put aside on the buffet for the moment, we tracked the women through time, from the fall of the Alamo to the end of World War II.

It was almost a decade after I first talked with my mother about putting together a family cookbook when G.P. Putnam's Sons published the results of the mother-daughter project, the 460-page historical novel *True Women* that also became a CBS mini-series.

When the book came out, I was interviewed on NBC's "Today Show," *True Women* received a very favorable write-up in the *New York Times Book Review* and the *Washington Post*, dozens of newspapers carried a nice story from the Associated Press, and it was fun to see my picture in *People* magazine. Later *True Women* was released as an Ivy Books paperback by the Ballantine division of Random House. And I must confess that I enjoyed my 15 minutes of fame.

When I was touring to promote my book, I spoke to groups all across the country, from Jacksonville, Florida, to Portland, Oregon. I would usually tell how the project began, and the story of the family cookbook that grew into a historical novel always seemed to please my audiences. But as Sarah said in *True Women*, "You can't fly so far your tail won't follow." So it seemed that after each appearance someone would approach me and ask, with politeness barely masking the eager impatience, "And when will your cookbook be coming out?"

Now, here at last, is the *True Women Cookbook* that started it all. ❧

The Bettie King Homeplace

"**M**y brother and I were blessed to grow up with wonderful parents, the best of a small-town childhood—a yard with a swing, a playhouse and a sandpile, collie dogs, and quarter horses grazing in our yard, second-hand pickups to drive, a beautiful clear spring nearby, fields of wild-flowers, a big barn, grandparents and aunts and uncles, and cousins to play with, living just down the road.

Memories of a wonderful old family home . . . Grandma's House."

My mother, Virginia Woods, lives in our family homeplace in Seguin, Texas. It was the home of her grandmother, Bettie Moss King, from the day she married in 1887 until the day she died in 1945, just after the end of World War II. When I was a little girl, our family—my father, Wilton Woods, my mother, Virginia, and my little brother Wilton—moved there. My great grandmother Bettie King had lived in the house for over half a century, and now Mother has lived there for more than half a century as well.

Mother calls the house at 920 East Court Street the Bettie King home. But my mother has lived there since early in 1946, so no one would be wrong to call it the Virginia Woods home. All my Seguin friends call it Janice's home because I lived there from the third grade until my second year of college. Probably my children and grandchildren have it right. They call it "Grandma's House."

Bettie and the man she would always call "Mr. Henry" were married in a double wedding along with her sister Nuge and the prosperous young businessman named Tom Lay.

Double wedding photographs of Bettie Moss King, left, and Sarah Nugent Moss Lay.

14

It is what a "Grandma's House" should be—welcoming, comfortable, dignified, but not formal, a house full of treasures for a grandma to explain to her grandchild. It was "Grandma's House" to my mother too, because when she was growing up, she spent every summer at Grandma's House.

It seems quite fitting and natural that *True Women* was conceived in Grandma's House. During the decade since then I flew from El Paso on Southwest Airlines once or twice a month to work on the book at the dining room table. There, Mother and I gathered research materials, interviewed relatives and family friends, wrote and rewrote scenes and dialogue and finally read the chapters aloud over and over until we agreed that I had it right.

In my book *True Women*, Bettie King is one of the three main characters. When the miniseries was filmed, she was one of 130 or so characters with speaking parts. In *True Women* I called this Bettie's house—because Mother always calls it the Bettie King house.

If time is a river, it flows deep through this house, and Bettie King's great carved-oak dining room table carried me and my mother on our voyage back into history. Over the years those generous boards have been the center of countless Sunday and holiday dinners, wedding receptions, fraternity reunions, political events, and family gatherings—like parties we called the Cousins' Club.

Bettie's husband, whom she always called "Mr. Henry," was critically injured when his wagon loaded with cotton overturned. Dr. Stamps came to the house and set his broken bones on the very same dining room table where Mother and I wrote *True Women*.

Texas actress Morgana Shaw, who played Bettie Moss in the film.

It is what a "Grandma's House" should be—welcoming, comfortable, dignified, but not formal, a house full of treasures for a grandma to explain to her grandchild.

Without fail, every Sunday evening promptly at seven, as predictable as the coming of night itself, Mary Lou found the time to ring up Bettie on the telephone. Bettie's telephone was a clearinghouse for all the news and information concerning the life and times of Seguin, Texas.

The table was Bettie's writing desk. A loyal correspondent, she sent letters filled with news of family, friends, and community to her far-flung kinfolk, always signing them, "Lovingly yours, Bettie King." She used the table at other times to lay out fabric to piece into quilts.

When I was growing up, Daddy—Wilton Woods—used the table as an office for his contracting business, often cluttering one end with an adding machine, a checkbook, piles of papers, and rolls of blueprints. From the other end of the table he might be running some campaign operation for his lifelong friend, Lyndon Baines Johnson.

Later on, Daddy made an office in the old smokehouse. Then Mother took over the table, with second-grade lesson plans opened in one place, papers to grade stacked in another. My brother and I would do our homework in a space cleared from our parents' paperwork.

All the papers would be moved out of sight in a jiffy when the table was needed to serve a group of family members or friends. The broad leaves would be added, a cloth draped over the long table, and that cloth topped with white damask or a crocheted overlay. A wonderful spread of food would appear, covering the table and the matching buffet beside it. The recipes for those home-cooked dishes drew on the family heritage of southern, Texan, and German cooking, and the popular regional cuisine know as Tex-Mex.

I have told you about Bettie King and her home in *True Women*. Let me tell you something about my own mother, Virginia Woods, and her home. It is hard to say where Bettie King's story ends and Mother's begins, especially when telling about the family home, but we can start my mother's story with her own mother's wedding.

On Christmas Day in 1910, Virginia King and William A. Bergfeld were married in front of the handmade mantelpiece in

Miss Mary Lou Lannom, one of "The Girls"

Virginia King Bergfeld

Bettie King's parlor. The service was performed by Brother T.J. Dodson, who had performed the ceremony for Virginia's parents Bettie and Henry 23 years before. Virginia and William rode to the depot in an open touring car, one of the town's first automobiles hired for the special occasion. They took their honeymoon at the Menger Hotel in San Antonio, just as her parents had done.

My mother's parents, Virginia and Will Bergfeld, lived a while in Weinert, Texas, a small farming town not far from Fort Worth. Mother's older sister, Mary Louise, was born there in 1912. In 1914, as the clouds of war gathered over Europe, Virginia King Bergfeld gave birth to a second baby girl and named her — Virginia.

When Mother was a toddler, the family moved back to Seguin. At first they lived at her grandmother Bettie King's house while her father built coastal defenses during World War I. When the war ended, the young family rented a house a few blocks away on Court Street.

Mother remembers being quarantined at her grandmother's house because she had the whooping cough. She couldn't live with her parents because her mother was pregnant. Mother was just four, sitting on the

On Christmas Day in 1910, Virginia King and William A. Bergfeld were married in front of the handsome mantelpiece in Bettie King's parlor.

Jennie Scott Hodges, one of "The Girls"

porch steps, when her Grandma came up and said, "You have a little
sister—Annie Maxine."

Mother had begun first grade in Seguin when her parents moved
to Moulton, a small town a few miles east of the Peach Creek homestead
of Sarah McClure Braches. There, Mother and her sisters, Mary Louise
and Annie Maxine, were joined by a baby brother, William, and then
another one, Henry Edsel.

Mother returned to Seguin every summer and stayed at the Bettie
King home. Her grandmother always brought her up to date on the
news about family and friends. Year after year, in the long summer
evenings, Bettie King sat on the porch entertaining Mother with yarns
about her family. Almost every day, Mother went to the house always
known as Euphemia's new house, and Aunt Annie told the stories once
more, as she had heard them from her own mother, Euphemia, in that
very house, and as they had been told by her Aunt Sarah at Peach Creek.

When company came to call it was time to share the stories again.
Bettie Moss King's younger brothers and sisters had lived with her and
"Mr. Henry" after the death of their mother, Mollie Moss. They moved
on by the time my mother was visiting, but when family came home,
Mother got to know her many aunts and uncles and cousins. Often
the visitors far outnumbered the beds available. When that happened,
quilts were stacked on the floor to make pallets.

Bettie's most regular visits came from the circle of women she
called "The Girls"—her sister Nuge, her sister-in-law Annie, Cayloma
Douglass, Mary Lou Lannom, and Jennie Scott Hodges. Sometimes
they had quilting bees, and other times she invited them over for a
"Spend the Day." They sat on the front porch or in the dining room
with their handwork of whatever kind—crocheting, knitting, darning
socks, patching clothes, or piecing quilts. The Girls reported the news
about their families and mutual friends while they worked, and often they

*Bettie King and Cayloma Douglass
at age twenty*

*Cayloma and Bettie
on Bettie's 75th birthday*

Bettie King's house was full of renters, mostly her nephews and their close friends. One friend, Virgil Halm, started dating Mother's sister, Maxine. After they married, Maxine and Virgil Halm lived for several years in the front bedroom of Bettie's house.

told stories handed down from their mothers and grandmothers. Nugent Moss Lay, Bettie's younger sister, had moved with her husband from a farm to a ranch to another ranch, each one more remote and desolate. Nuge's own everyday life was so forlorn, she loved to tell the family lore.

During the Great Depression of the thirties, Mother finished high school in Moulton as the salutatorian, but she was unable to go on to college or find a permanent job. In 1933, after Mr. Henry died, she spent a last summer living with her Grandma Bettie. In the winter of 1935, Mother's parents moved back to Seguin. Bettie King's house was full of renters, mostly her nephews—Mother's cousins, including Joe Fleming, and their close friends. One friend, Virgil Halm, started dating Mother's sister Maxine when she moved to Seguin. After they married, Maxine and Virgil Halm lived for several years in the front bedroom of Bettie's house.

Mother was finally able to land a student job for the fall semester of 1934 at Southwest Texas State in San Marcos. She needed $50 to enroll, but neither she nor her parents had the cash. Bettie King gave her the needed money.

Mother went to college for 12 months, straight through summer, until she got a temporary teaching certificate. She found a job in Stewart's Prairie, a tiny community in Gonzales County. She had a room and took her meals with the family of the school board chairman, while she taught as many as 50 students in six grades in a one-room schoolhouse.

In the spring of 1936 she became engaged to Wilton Woods, who had finished Southwest Texas College a few years before her. He and Lyndon Johnson had been among the seven founding members of the White Star fraternity at that college, and it was L.B.J. who stood up to announce the engagement at the annual reunion of the White Stars.

But my mother was worried. What could they do about a wedding,

when no one they knew had money for an

elegant service, for fancy food or clothes, or

even presents? To make her wedding

something special without imposing on

their hard-pressed families and friends, they

borrowed a car from Willard Deason, another

White Star founder, and drove out to Marfa

in West Texas where the long-retired Baptist preacher, Brother T.J.

Dodson, the same minister who had performed the rites of marriage for

my great grandmother, Bettie Moss King, and later for my grandmoth-

er, was to carry on the family tradition by intoning the ritual for my mother

and father.

Mother always laughs when she tells how proud Brother Dodson

was to be asked to perform this third generation wedding ceremony. In

his excitement, he became a bit confused. When the distinguished cler-

gyman came to the closing prayer, he commenced the service all over

again, but Virginia and Wilton stood patiently and repeated their wedding

vows. When Brother Dodson for a second time began the closing prayer,

his wife tugged on his sleeve and said, "That's the end now. Stop."

Three years later in San Antonio, with war clouds gathering once

again over Europe, Mother gave birth to a baby girl, and I was born.

At the time, Daddy was working for the Railroad Commission in

San Antonio. Not long after I was born, Mother and Daddy moved to

Waco, where he worked on the 1940 Census. In Corpus Christi he was

the head of personnel for Brown & Root, the contractor on the Naval

Air Station. We were living in Austin when my brother Wilton was born in 1944. In a short period we had a dozen different addresses, but the Bettie King house was always home. I was eight years old when my grandmother, Bettie King, died in 1945 at the age of 80, and a few months later we moved into her home.

All the years I was growing up, Mother was teaching us history. My parents' idea of a family vacation was to put my brother and me in the car, and, while Daddy drove, Mother read history books aloud to him and to the captive audience in the back seat. We went down the highways stopping at every roadside historical marker.

Whenever we visited family, we took in historical sites nearby. A trip to see my Aunt Mary Louise and Uncle Billie Orr included the port of Jefferson, where Mississippi River steamboats stopped. Going to Corpus Christi, where my Uncle Henry Edsel Bergfeld and Aunt Bernice were living, we detoured to see the missions at Goliad as well. When my Uncle Bill Bergfeld, Jr. and Aunt Elsie settled in Conroe, we soon visited Sam Houston's home in Huntsville.

The year I was finishing high school, Mother began teaching second grade in a classroom in the same building where she had started first grade 35 years before. Mother, like her mother before her, had been taught by the formidable and beloved woman for whom the institution is now named, Mary B. Erskine.

Mother spends more time in her comfortable home now that she is retired. She has kept it much the same as it was when her grandma, Bettie, and her grandpa, Henry King, lived out their lives there. Now she enjoys showing family and friends around the house.

Bettie Moss King said that the first time she saw

Wilton Woods and his infant son,
Wilton Eugene in 1945.

Virginia Woods

their new house, she was driving her buggy on the way to be fitted for her wedding dress when she passed the King farm. She pulled up the horse's reins for a moment and watched Henry, her husband-to-be, and a friend, builder William C. Thomas, hammering the rough-hewn lumber on the side of what would be their new home.

Not long ago, we found her hand-embroidered wedding night-gown packed away in tissue paper. It is a treasured family keepsake.

The house, with its big high windows across the front and east side, breathes with tranquillity. Originally the house had only three rooms. Two rooms were on the west side and one on the east with a dog-trot between them. Later, the dog-trot—an open-ended passage between two sections of the house once common to most all Texas houses—became the central entrance hall. A long dining room was added behind the single room and a kitchen was attached behind.

Mother calls the house at 920 East Court Street the Bettie King home. But my mother has lived there since 1946, so no one would be wrong to call it the Virginia Woods home.

Finally, John Goodrum, a local builder, added the columned Greek Revival-style porch across the front. The two-story barn to the east of the house is probably the largest wooden building in Seguin, if not in the county.

Bettie's husband, "Mr. Henry," worked with three tenant farmers. The mules were changed for fresh teams when the men came in for lunch. In other words, the mules worked hard for half a day, while Henry King and the tenant farmers worked from sunup to sundown. Every year, Abe Miller, one of the tenants, drove a matched team of well-trained mules in the Juneteenth parade that was followed by a picnic under the Capote Road bridge over the Guadalupe River. Bettie King always baked three of her lemon jelly cakes for the tenant families to take to the Juneteenth picnic.

When Mother was little, a play house in the backyard held child-sized furniture made by "Mr. Henry" for my mother's mother when she was a young girl. As a child, my own mother delighted in lying down in the tiny hand-turned spool bed. But Bettie King was a practical woman, and when grandchildren outgrew those toys, she converted the playhouse into a chicken coop for her biddy hens.

The chicken coop was gone by the time we moved into Bettie's house, so Daddy built a new playhouse for me. It was the meeting place of many of my girlfriends, serving at various times as a doll hospital, a fortress, a tea house, and even as a beauty shop where my friends—the future True Women of Seguin—could practice rolling hair, wearing bras and putting on lipstick.

Idella said, "A president of the United States will be welcome in your home. You're a mighty lucky woman, Bettie King. Your house will outlive your great-great grandchildren."

The playhouse was all but abandoned one year in the 1950's when my father was host to a barbecue, a reunion of the White Star fraternity. His oldest and dearest friends—easily 50 or 60 of them—were gathered in the backyard, where a spread of beef, chicken, and sausage, along with pinto beans, potato salad, sliced dill pickles, and corn bread, were ready to be served.

Suddenly the crowd moved as if a shot had been fired. Men began hurrying toward the front yard, and others rushed into the house. I ran to the front yard and saw the biggest, longest, black Cadillac that I had ever seen just behind a highway patrol car flashing a red light.

The men had run to the porch, crowding into the front door, so I ran around to the back door to try to get ahead of them.

About that time Lyndon Johnson came through the house into the backyard, moving steadily from one outstretched hand to another, passing a word or two with one old friend, and dropping his long arms around another. He saw me, swooped me up and said, "Janice, how's my girl?"

Then he moved on.

I turned my attention back to the barbecue. After all, I was a jaded high school student who had seen Lyndon Johnson many, many times before, even if of late it had mostly been in ballroom receiving lines or on platforms at campaign rallies. So I was quite surprised to see Daddy open the door to my old playhouse while Senator Johnson, Bill Deason, Fenner Roth, and Ernest Morgan ducked inside.

What was going on—five grown men in my playhouse?

I ran to look in the window, but all I could see was Lyndon Johnson talking while the men listened. I caught some angry words about a man named Joe McCarthy, but I did not know what they were talking about. When they came out, L.B.J. stopped to tell Mother that he could not stay because he had business in San Antonio. He reached

When Mother was little, a playhouse in the backyard held child-sized furniture made by "Mr. Henry." As a child, Mother delighted in lying down in the tiny hand-turned spool bed.

One day Daddy brought home a collie dog we named Laddie, and he was as handsome and intelligent as an example of the breed could be, and far too smart to be stopped by any fence that Daddy could build.

over and patted my shoulder. Trailing White Stars behind him, the Majority Leader of the United States Senate walked across our front yard, got back into the big Cadillac, and left.

I guess I will never know what L.B.J. and Daddy and their friends talked about in those moments they huddled in my playhouse. Daddy was the kind of man who would never tell a secret he promised to keep. Never.

Every spring during the 10 or 12 years that Daddy was a successful home builder, he arranged for a dump truck load of sand to be delivered back by the fig tree. We would turn on a slow-running water hose. This was in those simple days when water was cheap and plentiful. My brother Wilton—we all called him Woody until he grew up and moved to New York City—and I could play in the sand, spending hours and hours transforming the sandy desert into castles and palaces amid canals and lakes and peopled them with assorted dolls and plastic warriors. Mother and Daddy removed one or two scoops of the sand at a time for her flower beds and his tomato garden. By the time winter arrived, our sandpile was gone.

One day Daddy brought home a collie we named Laddie, and he was as handsome and intelligent as an example of the breed could be, and far too smart to be stopped by any fence that Daddy could build. He went over if he could, or under if he had to, though he did not like to get his beautiful golden coat dirty. Laddie seemed bound to roam, apparently answering the call of lonesome females all across the town.

Laddie died about the time Wayne and I were married. By the time I had children, Daddy had brought home another collie he called Sassy. She was a beauty, too, her dark coat highlighted with gold and white markings and, apparently, the kind of lonesome female that caused dogs like Laddie to roam.

Virginia Woods with Laddie

Each summer my children—Wayne, Virginia, and Charles would stay at Grandma's house just in time to play with a new litter of puppies. After the grandchildren left, Daddy would give the puppies away.

Nowadays, when I drive around Seguin, it seems that half the dogs in town are part collie, some golden-haired like Laddie, and others dark like Sassy.

The grandchildren also enjoyed the patented version of the family vacation. Each one sat in the car, with Mother reading history books aloud to Daddy—and the captive audience in the back seat. Of course, Daddy had read most of these books before. *Thirteen Days to Glory*, the classic on the Battle of the Alamo, was one of their favorites for these readings.

Years before his retirement, when Daddy's building business had been prospering, he bought himself a horse. Soon he had five. He kept them for a while in a pen he built by the barn. Daddy grew up on a Hill Country ranch and learned to ride a horse before he could walk. He liked to say that horseback riding had given him a sense of balance and rhythm. He especially loved his mare Mitzi, and later he rode her filly, June Princess, with the Guadalupe County Sheriff's Mounted Posse.

I always liked to go to the Friday night drills and hang on the

Wilton Woods on Mitzi

Daddy loved to ride his mare Mitzi with the Guadalupe County Sheriff's Mounted Posse. I always liked to go to the Friday night drills and hang on the arena fence and watch as the horsemen rode in fast-paced formations and practiced their daring trick riding.

"I see your home," Idella said. "Columns white as alabaster. A little boy playing in a sandpile in the yard. A man carefully tending his tomato vines. I see a young woman living there who looks just like you. And a little girl with Hawkins blue eyes growing up to be a woman in your house."

arena fence and watch as the horsemen rode in fast-paced formation and practiced their daring trick riding.

Mother still keeps an eye on the town of Seguin from the wide sweeping front porch, her favorite part of the house. At one end the Seven Sisters rose climbs as it always has, though it rarely blooms now that pecan trees have grown so large they cast their shade across it.

The soft coral pink flowers of the Queen's Crown vine drape over the other end of the porch. The porch is comfortable, inviting to everyone who wants to rest in the hottest days of summer. That's when I retreat inside the air-conditioned house. Mother likes to recall the days before air-conditioning, when the porch was the best spot to catch any breeze.

The front door of Bettie's house has panes of stained glass, characteristic of the Victorian period, admitting shafts of colored light to the paneled hallway that was once a dog-trot. The east room was her parlor. Here the old fireplace is still graced by the hand-carved mantel built by W.C. Kishbaugh. Bettie paid him with eggs, milk, butter, and bacon.

Framed postcards with illustrations of embracing couples now hang above the desk. They had been mailed from Will Bergfeld, my mother's father, to Virginia King when she was at Kidd Key College in Sherman, Texas. Even receiving letters from a man was forbidden then, so somehow they had been smuggled past the college censor. Long after her parents had died, my mother found the colorful post-cards and had them framed.

A light oak oval table stands in a corner. It came from my father's family. By tradition, it was made by Ed Tom Lawshe, the slave son of Captain Lewis Lawshe, the captain who was also the father of Georgia Lawshe Woods. The Woods family ranching brand is burned into the underside of the tabletop.

At Christmastime, Bettie King put a small tree on a round table in the center of her parlor, and kept the pocket doors closed until it was time to open the presents. The children always tried to peek through the keyholes, but could only catch a sparkle or two from the shiny candy wrappers and the mercury-glass ornaments on the tree.

The pocket doors still slide into the wall and open into the dining room. The table where Mother and I worked on *True Women* is large enough to seat 16 adults comfortably, or 20 with a squeeze.

The most striking feature is the flooring made of soft pine boards that run uncut from end to end, each one 24 feet in length. The center hall also opens into the dining room, through a double-width arched entryway. Taken together, the hallway, dining room, and living room are ready to welcome a large gathering, just as they always have.

Henry King

Not long after we moved into the house, Mother's younger brother, Henry Edsel Bergfeld, almost always called Edsie, decided to marry Bernice Phillips. My grandmother, Virginia Bergfeld, had her heart set on having the wedding reception in the parlor of Bettie King's house where she had married Edsie's father, William A. Bergfeld.

My own mother was appalled. A few major restorations had been made to the house since the Depression began, but that was 15 years earlier. So much still needed to be done.

The furniture was moved—some to the porch, some to the back of the house. Fortunately, no rain fell to loosen the new wallpaper. The wainscoting was cleaned, and the floors were refinished. The guests at the wedding reception exclaimed how nice the old house looked.

When Congressman Lyndon B. Johnson was locked in a make-or-break race for the U.S. Senate, the house was a showplace when

Jonathan Brent, the actor
who played Henry King

Abe Miller

Mother held a tea for the candidate's wife. But Guadalupe County was not L.B.J. country. Descendants of the German-American Unionists were still voting Republican, and the local oil-money Democrats had never been part of the Roosevelt-Johnson wing of the party.

Nevertheless, Mother was the granddaughter of Bettie Moss King, and her guest list filled the venerable house with women who came to have a piece of Hawkins Plantation cake and meet Lady Bird Johnson.

Perhaps the most sentimental of the parties held in these rooms were the somewhat regular meetings of the Cousins' Club. While attending still another sad funeral, someone had the refreshing idea that the family should get together for the sake of getting together, not only for funerals. A group of cousins organized, set a date, and invited everyone descended from Bettie King's parents. Over a decade or so, the Cousins' Club reunions were held in several towns across South Texas about twice a year, but the feelings seemed strongest when we all gathered at Bettie King's house, the old family home.

A trundle bed from the log cabin of Euphemia and William King, "Mr. Henry's" parents, is in Bettie's front bedroom. Through the years, that trundle bed has been pulled out and used for many children, and sometimes adults.

In the back bedroom, Mother's closets have replaced the old wardrobes. Bettie had two big closets put in her bedroom during the Depression when she was renting out her other rooms and needed storage space. As a practical woman she did not waste her limited cash on such frills as hardware. A threadspool became the doorknob, and the closet door was held shut by turning a small piece of wood, like closing a fence gate. Mother has kept it just that way.

She also likes to show where her grandma hid behind the door in that bedroom during a storm.

We moved into the homeplace when I was an impressionable third-grader. One day Abe Miller, the old tenant farmer who had worked for Mr. Henry, was working in the yard while I was playing outside. A rumble of thunder in the afternoon heat drove me onto the porch. I sat in Grandma Bettie's rocker while he began tell me a ghost story.

"Miss Bettie always had such a terrible fear of storms," he said. "She'd go in that very back bedroom where you sleep at nights. She'd hide in the corner and pray. When a storm comes, if you look in the corner of your room, you'll see Miss Bettie's ghost asking the Lord to let the storm pass by."

I ran to tell my Mother that Abe had said my Grandma King was a ghost in my bedroom. She did not want me to be afraid of ghosts or anything else, so she said, "Well, I hope you do see her ghost. My

One day Abe Miller, the old tenant farmer who had worked for "Mr. Henry," was working in the yard when he stopped to tell me a ghost story.

grandmother Bettie King was the loveliest woman you ever could know. And if you do see her, be sure and tell her who you are."

When I began my research to write about Bettie King, I had to find out what had caused her to have such a profound fear of storms, so profound that everyone who had known her talked about it.

I learned the answer from Leonard Moss Fisher, who lived in Port Lavaca and was 92 years old. He was Bettie King's nephew who was also a grandson and namesake of her father, "Papa" Leonard Moss.

When Leonard Fisher was a teenager, he said, it was his duty once a year to drive his grandfather to the gulf coast to a place not far from the now bygone port of Indianola. There, in a grove of trees, "Papa" Leonard had buried his father and mother when he was only a little boy. On one of these trips, "Papa" Leonard told his grandson the awful fears he had carried throughout his life.

Making their way from the coast during an epidemic of yellow fever, his mother, his father, and a brother had died. Young Leonard and his other brother, who was also sick, tried to bury them, but they were far too weak to dig deeply. No one would help them for fear of catching the fever.

Later, "Papa" Leonard saw other shallow graves that had been ripped open, the bodies mutilated by wolves. At night he heard howls, and through the fever that filled his head, he had gruesome visions of wolves unearthing the bodies of his loved ones.

"Papa" Leonard told his grandson, Leonard Fisher, that years later, when a tornado had killed a neighboring family on the Capote Road, those awful thoughts had come flooding back. He made his young daughter Bettie guard those bodies and stoke a fire to be sure no wolves did

After the storm, he looked out into the darkness where the wolves were gathering. "Can't just leave 'em for the wolves. You'll just have to do it. Keep feeding the fire, Bettie. I won't be gone long. You're a strong girl, you can do it."

George Henry King

them harm. With tears in his eyes, Papa Leonard said, "Every human being is entitled to a decent burial."

As I began to write *True Women*, I tried to retrace and refresh the oral history that has been handed down to me. I often found particular missing pieces, as I did when Leonard Moss Fisher told about his grandfather and the wolves. I could never have guessed that wolves had anything to do with Bettie King.

On occasion, working at the dining room table, Mother and I would come to a dead end. It was then, in the quiet of the evening, that I felt the spirits of true women moving to push the book *True Women* to its completion.

One weekend toward the end of the writing, we were struggling with the section about Bettie King. It was long after I had sent the first manuscripts of the sections on Euphemia and Georgia Lawshe Woods to Neil Nyren, my editor at G.P. Putnam's Sons in New York, and I was really feeling the deadline pressure.

George Henry King's story, for instance, had big holes. I hated to leave it that way, but I knew nothing about the type of combat in which George Henry had been killed. How could I write a descriptive scene without talking to someone who knew him? How could I write about a

"Dear Grandmother," George Henry wrote, "My morale has been kept high by receiving letters regularly from you. We had a large Christmas tree all decorated with lights just like dear old Seguin used to have."

woman's life without talking about the birth—and finally the death—of a grandchild born in her home?

I had a childhood memory of being at the depot in Seguin when something sad was happening, but not understanding what it was. Now I was a grownup and I still did not know about the battles before George Henry's body came home from World War II in a flag-draped coffin.

My husband Wayne called me early one morning from our home in El Paso. I told him I was trying to write about George Henry's death but I knew nothing about his wartime experiences. Jokingly, I told Wayne I was walking around the house with my arms outstretched, imploring the spirits, "Tell me what happened to George Henry King."

Joe Fleming at the grave of his cousin, George Henry King.

Within an hour of that conversation the doorbell rang.

I opened the door to find a stranger on the porch. He said his name was Allen Hoermann, and he asked if this was the King home. I said, "Yes, my mother lives here and years ago it was the home of my great-grandmother, Bettie King."

"Well, I'm only in town for the day, because tonight is the 50th reunion of our high school class," he said. "As I drove from Thrall toward Seguin I had an overpowering feeling to check on the King family because my best friend in high school was George Henry King. You know in World War II we joined the Marines together, and I was with him when he was killed."

When I regained my composure, I invited Allen in to sit at Bettie King's dining room table. My heart was pounding as I asked him to tell what happened in the Pacific combat. Allen gave a gripping description of dreadful jungle fighting in the Russell Islands, near Guadalcanal, against enemy soldiers tied high in the tops of palm trees. Allen said George Henry fell wounded beside him; there was blood everywhere, and they carried him away.

Naturally, I used his vivid war stories about George Henry King. So the man who came to the door of Bettie's house became a character in her own story.

I know Bettie King wanted Allen Hoermann included in *True Women*. It seems to me she called him to her home—and invited him inside.

In 1983, my father died. Losing him, and thinking about my family and our history inspired me to write about it. And so I began *True Women*.

It made me appreciate what my family has shared. My brother and I were blessed to grow up with wonderful parents, the best of a small-town childhood—a yard with a swing, a playhouse, and a sandpile, collie dogs and quarter horses, a beautiful clear spring nearby, fields of wildflowers, a big barn, grandparents, aunts, uncles, and cousins to play with, living just down the road.

Memories of a wonderful old family home . . . Grandma's House.

In 1983, my father died. Losing him, and thinking about my family and our history inspired me to write about it. And so I began *True Women.*

Chicken Ham Salad

"ENOUGH FOR COXEY'S ARMY."

Servings: 34

2   chickens, boiled,
     meat removed
1 1/2 pounds ham cubes,
     from cooked ham
2   dozen eggs, hard-boiled
1   quart chopped garlic dill
     pickles (relish)
2   large onions, chopped
4   celery ribs, chopped
1   tablespoon dry mustard
1 1/2 pounds sauerkraut
     salt and pepper to taste

Chop chicken meat and place in very large bowl. Add ham cubes. Remove yolk from egg whites. Mash yolks and chop whites. Add to meat mixture and combine. Add relish, onion, celery, mustard, and sauerkraut, and mix. Taste and adjust seasonings using vinegar from relish, and salt and pepper to taste.

To boil chicken: Clean chickens and rub skin with a mixture of salt, pepper, and paprika. Also, place seasonings and garlic cloves in between skin and meat of chicken, massaging into chicken meat. Put chickens in a large pot with one large sliced onion, one large sliced lemon, salt and pepper. Cover chickens with water and bring to a boil. Immediately turn down heat and allow to simmer until meat falls off the bone, about 1 1/2 to 2 hours.

PREP TIME FOR CHICKENS: 20 minutes.
COOK TIME: 1 1/2 - 2 hours.

PREP TIME FOR SALAD: 1 1/4 hours.
ASSEMBLY TIME
FOR SALAD: 15 minutes.

TESTED RECIPE

PER SERVING: 200 CALORIES ❦ 11G FAT (48% CALORIES FROM FAT) ❦ 14G PROTEIN
12G CARBOHYDRATES ❦ 72MG CHOLESTEROL ❦ 643MG SODIUM

Lemon Jelly Cake

"FOR MR. HENRY"

FOR CAKE: Preheat oven to 375 degrees. Cream shortening, and add sugar slowly, beating well. Add unbeaten eggs, one at a time, beating well after each egg is added. Add lemon juice. Sift together dry ingredients and add alternately with milk to first mixture. Bake in two greased, floured layer-cake pans. Bake in 375 degree oven for 20 to 25 minutes.

FOR ICING: Combine ingredients in saucepan and cook over high heat whisking constantly. Allow icing to come to a boil and cook for 1 minute, continuing to whisk. Allow mixture to cool about 10 to 15 minutes before icing cake. Icing will thicken as it cools. Once cooled, icing will harden and form a crust.

TO ASSEMBLE: Place one layer on a platter, top side up, and ice. Place other layer on top of iced layer, top side up, and ice. For cake baked in springform pan, allow cake to cool. Open springform and ice cake. Decorate just before serving. ❧

CAKE PREP TIME: 30 minutes.
COOK TIME: 25 minutes.
ICING PREP TIME: 10 minutes.
COOK TIME: 5 minutes.
TO ASSEMBLE AND ICE: 10 minutes.

Servings: 14

1/2	cup shortening
1	cup sugar
2	eggs
1	teaspoon baking powder
1/4	teaspoon salt
2/3	cup milk
3	tablespoons lemon juice
2	cups sifted cake flour

Icing:

1	cup sugar
1	egg
1	tablespoon water
1	teaspoon flour
1	lemon, juiced with grated rind

OPTION: For one-layer cake use springform pan.

TESTED RECIPE

PER SERVING: 258 CALORIES ❧ 9G FAT (30% CALORIES FROM FAT) ❧ 3G PROTEIN ❧ 43G CARBOHYDRATE
40MG CHOLESTEROL ❧ 82MG SODIUM

Runaway Wedding Cake

"BAKED FOR JESSIE ELKINS AND JOHN MOSS'S ELOPEMENT"

Preheat oven to 350 degrees. Cream butter and sugar thoroughly, about 3 minutes. In another bowl, combine flour and baking powder. In a third bowl, mix pineapple juice and lemon juice with pineapple fruit, applesauce and marmalade. Add the fruit and juice mixture to the butter/sugar mixture, alternating with the flour/baking powder mixture. Add almond extract and mix. In a clean bowl, beat egg whites until stiff peaks form. Fold the beaten egg whites into the batter, and then carefully fold in the coconut, cherries and almonds so as not to deflate the batter. Bake in a well-greased tube pan (bundt pan) for 1 hour and 30 minutes or until a toothpick inserted into thickest part of cake comes out with moist crumbs. Remove from oven and let stand in pan for 4 hours before removing.

Servings:
24

3/4	cup butter, softened
1 1/2	cups sugar
3	cups flour
5	teaspoons baking powder
1	cup pineapple juice
1/4	cup lemon juice
1/2	cup pineapple, chopped and drained
1/2	cup applesauce, unsweetened
1/2	cup orange marmalade
1	teaspoon almond extract
6	egg whites
1	cup coconut, shredded
1	pound maraschino cherries, drained
1	cup almonds, chopped

PREP TIME: 1 hour 10 minutes.
COOK TIME: 1 hour 30 minutes.

TESTED RECIPE

Per serving: 250 Calories ❧ 10g Fat (34% calories from fat) ❧ 4g Protein
39g Carbohydrate ❧ 15mg Cholesterol ❧ 162mg Sodium

Miss Bettie's Tea Cakes

"FOR THE GIRLS"

FOR CAKE: Preheat oven to 350 degrees. Stir lemon juice into milk. Set aside to sour. In a mixing bowl, combine flour, baking soda, baking powder and salt. Add milk/ juice mixture and stir. Add egg and lemon peel and stir. Add sugar slowly. Batter will be stiff. Drop by teaspoons onto UNGREASED aluminum or stainless-steel baking sheet 3 inches apart. Bake for 12 minutes. Remove from baking sheet with a spatula while the cakes are still hot. Cool, then top with icing.

FOR ICING: Combine powdered sugar, lemon juice, and melted butter. Whisk until smooth.

CAKE PREP TIME: 35 minutes.
BAKE TIME: 12 minutes.
ICING PREP TIME: 10 minutes.
ICE TIME: 10 minutes per batch.

The batter for these tea cakes is very stiff.
Use a free-standing mixer, not a hand mixer,
when making the batter.

Servings: 40

2	teaspoons lemon juice
1/2	cup milk
1/2	cup butter
1 3/4	cups all-purpose flour
1	teaspoon baking soda
1	teaspoon baking powder
1/2	teaspoon salt
1	egg
1	teaspoon lemon peel, finely shredded
3/4	cup sugar

Icing:

1 3/4	cups sifted powdered sugar
2	tablespoons lemon juice
1	tablespoon melted butter
2	drops yellow food coloring, optional

TESTED RECIPE

Per serving: 81 Calories ❦ 3g Fat (31% calories from fat) ❦ 1g Protein ❦ 13g Carbohydrate
12mg Cholesterol ❦ 96mg Sodium

Sarah's Great House at Peach Creek

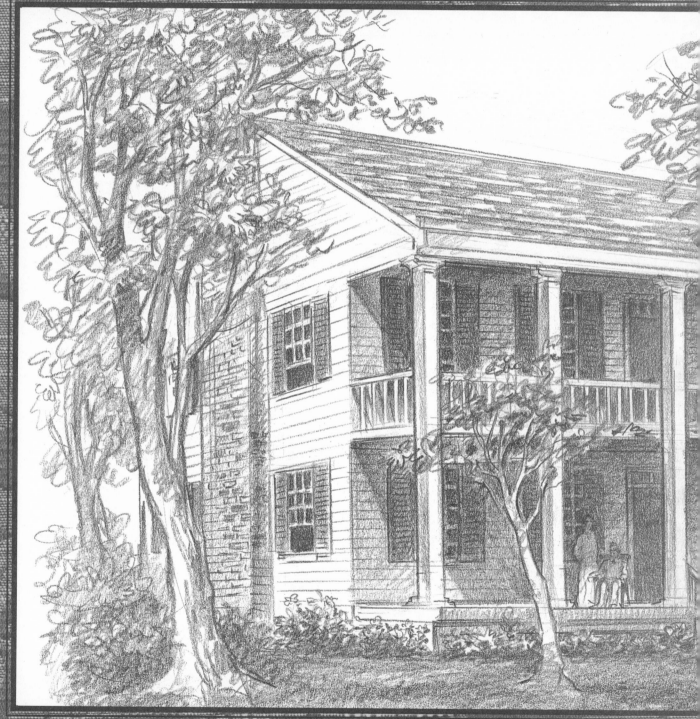

"Down there," Sarah said, "by that grove of wild plums, will be the grandest house this side of New Orleans. Tall white columns and everything."

"Can I try your pipe?" Euphemia asked.

"May I," corrected Sarah.

"May I try your pipe?"

"Of course not!"

"You smoke."

"You're not me," Sarah said. "It's time for change. I'd like to build a place that isn't so hard and mean. We've been so busy just surviving, we don't have time to be human."

A few weeks after I began working on my plan for a family cookbook, Mother took me back to visit Sarah's great house. Years before I had seen it as a child, but Mother told me if I were to do something with the family history, I had to see where it all began.

From my hometown of Seguin we drove along Capote Road toward Gonzales, and then we continued east on Highway 90-A to Peach Creek. The familiar route carried us through Texas scenery the way I always picture it. Gently rolling hills of sand and loam were covered by wildflowers, each field more spectacular than the last. All along the roadside the white country houses glowed in the spring warmth, their friendly porches done up with gingerbread frolics. Herds of Hereford cattle leisurely grazed the sun-splashed lush of the sprouting grasses. The live oaks were already filling out with the new season's greenery, and in the verdant brush the mesquite trees sported fine new leaves in sweet tines of chartreuse.

Frederick Law Olmsted, America's greatest landscape architect, remarked upon the richness and beauty of scenes much like these in his book, *A Journey Through Texas*. Olmsted especially liked the open fields amid the stands of great oaks. He also noted that the earliest settlers located their rude houses in the most beautiful spot on their land—usually a place shaded by fine trees but beside a sunny meadow. Later, Olmsted followed this principle in his design for Central Park in New York, mixing rolling open spaces of meadows and lawns with groves of specimen trees.

Sarah, now nineteen, had been a mother to Euphemia since her own mother died. It was hard to imagine a real mother as extraordinary as Sarah: a beautiful woman who could ride like a Comanche and shoot as accurately as any man in Texas.

Sarah Ashby McClure Braches, painted by Anne Bell.

As we made our way through the classic Central Texas scenery, Mother and I talked about the woman who built the house we were going to see once again. Born Sarah Ann Ashby, she first married Bartlett McClure, and after his death she remarried, becoming known as Sarah McClure Braches. But in our family she was always called Aunt Sarah. We are descended from Sarah's baby sister, Euphemia, who was raised by Sarah as her own child after their parents died.

Many of the stories about Sarah and Euphemia and their pioneer family were passed on by Euphemia's daughter, always called Aunt Annie. We believed these stories were true because, they said, Aunt Sarah herself had pointed out the oak where she and Euphemia had seen Sam Houston on his white horse, Saracen. Aunt Sarah had bragged about outrunning Comanches by jumping her horse across a deep gully. She also had told about confronting a Comanche raiding party and saving her home and family. Of course, we all knew that Aunt Sarah with little Euphemia and the Widows of the Alamo — together with thousands of other women and children — had fled from Santa Anna's invading army in the Runaway Scrape. And at that time, we had heard, Aunt Sarah had tragically lost both her unborn child and her infant, Little Johnny.

We crossed the bridges over Peach Creek, turned at the roadside historical marker, and stopped at the pasture gate. From the road we could make out the magnificent Sam Houston Oak, but the old house we had come to see was lost in brush that had overgrown the area. Mother led the way back toward the creek until we reached Sarah's

Dana Delany, who played Sarah in the film.

"Men may be stronger, but there is power in being a woman," Sarah said.

Euphemia Texas Ashby King

"What can I do?" Euphemia asked.

"How can I change things?"

"Grow up to be a woman," Sarah

answered. "You can change this

world. Soften the edges of our lives."

great house. The house was almost in ruins, and yet it was still a vision of elegance and splendor. Though the paint had long ago weathered from its native lumber and the windows were boarded up, the house stood tall and proud, with wide double galleries supported by towering columns and chimneys at both ends. An old rose climbed along a fence, and abandoned milk and wine lilies grew in the yard. Giant oaks shaded it from the afternoon sun. Beyond the yard, wildflowers bloomed on the wide flood plain of Peach Creek and in patches among the oaks of the neighboring pasture.

The silent grandeur of the place moved me, and standing in the shade of her home, I knew Sarah had felt a passion for this beautiful land. Like other pioneer women, she had come to Texas, fallen in love with the place, and made it her home. And there at Peach Creek I began to realize that I was confronting something that was profound—though I did not imagine then what my little history project would become. But clearly, the life stories of pioneer women on the Texas frontier could not be contained in a few pages of family history layered between their recipes. At Peach Creek I felt my simple family cookbook begin to grow into the novel *True Women*.

Now I would have to gather the history and make it real. This visit was an important step. Here I had seen the evidence that Aunt Sarah returned to Peach Creek following the Battle of San Jacinto to start life anew. Here, too, I saw where Aunt Sarah was buried in the family plot with her first husband on one side of her and her second husband on the other side. I had made my pilgrimage to the home of our family matriarch, and I had heard the voice of Sarah, the original storyteller.

Soon afterward, I began what was to become years of research into the intertwined family and Texas history. I was relieved to find many sources supplying documentation to back up the family's oral history. Indeed, Sarah herself was frequently cited by John H. Brown, who wrote some of the earliest Texas histories.

Tina Majorino, who played little Euphemia.

The family Bible belonging to Hartwell Kennard, the great-great-grandson of Sarah McClure Braches, records the birth and death of the infant Little Johnny during the Runaway Scrape.

According to these accounts, the foundation of Sarah's great house was laid in 1839—a few years after she abandoned her log cabin in the Runaway Scrape—and the building was finished three years later. She supervised an itinerant housewright, who put up the frame and much of the walls, before he was scared away by a Comanche raid.

From the early years, the main house was surrounded by outbuildings, sheds, and corrals that provided shelter for their animals, and cabins for the slaves and visitors. Travelers from the old ports of Linneville and Indianola often passed this way and stopped here where they found fresh water, shade from the spreading oaks, and the wide inviting porches of the main house.

Sarah's husband Bartlett McClure died of exposure during a winter storm in 1842. The next year Charles Braches, an early immigrant from Germany, was serving in the Congress of the Republic of Texas. Braches stopped at the home of the widow Sarah McClure on his way to Houston, the temporary capital at the time, and he found reason to pass that way again, and then again.

Sarah's wedding to Charles Braches was held on March 2, 1843.

Powers Boothe, who played Bartlett McClure.

"She's your slave, Euphemia. You and your sisters inherited her like any other property, from your father. She does your washing, works in your garden and will care for our children," William said. Euphemia felt herself grow smaller.

The guests for this Texas Independence Day celebration of their union included family, friends, Congressmen, judges, and other dignitaries from far and wide. The parlor of Sarah's house was decorated with flowering branches from peach trees and bouquets of pink, red, and purple phlox and other early wildflowers in her fields.

Among the documents providing details of Sarah's life is a farm journal kept by Charles Braches. During the years before the Civil War he recorded the schedule of the stagecoaches, which stopped at Sarah's great house to change the teams of horses and to refresh the passengers. This stop was a half day's ride from Gonzales, and a full day from Columbus on the Colorado River, when a stagecoach ride between Houston and San Antonio took a grueling four days each way.

After all the years that I spent researching and writing *True Women*, I was disappointed that I found no monument erected to honor the women who helped to build Texas. The Alamo has been restored and preserved by the Daughters of the Republic of Texas to honor the brave men who fought and died there. The San Jacinto Monument proudly marks the battlefield where our freedom was won. But no shrine, no statue, no sacred place commemorates the strength and courage of the women who saved their families in the Runaway Scrape. No relics or vestiges exist of the heroic women of the Texas Republic, except, of course, for a few of their homes that have survived the years.

Today, more than a century and a half since it was built, the imposing home of Sarah McClure Braches calls to mind a fine plantation house—like the ones she knew growing up in Kentucky before her family moved to Texas in 1831.

Tildy Ashby

Visitors on the *True Women* tours to see Sarah's great house make a contribution to the local preservation group. These contributions have helped to pay for a significant restoration of this old house.

The brush has been cleared, and nowadays the house is readily seen from the road. New steps were built and the chimneys were stabilized, using stones taken from the original quarry a few miles away. The porches and interior floors have been repaired, broken windows replaced, the roof fixed, and a new coat of paint applied to protect the aged wooden walls. Visitors on escorted tours can go inside the house to the expansive attic room; there they look out across the tops of the surrounding oaks at a landscape of floodplain and pastureland dotted with hundreds of giant oaks. Little has changed from the way it was when the pioneers first settled here on the Texas frontier.

Not far from the house, under two immense live oaks, Sarah McClure Braches and her family lie beneath the original gravestones, in a small plot protected by a fence of wrought iron.

The home of Sarah Ann McClure Braches has become her enduring monument, and much more than that. Each year the Runaway Scrape is reenacted by the historical association of Gonzales and a picnic is held around the venerable Sam Houston Oak. The nearby family graveyard serves as a reminder of all the dead babies, children and husbands who were mourned by women on the frontier, and as a memorial to them. The historic site is a tribute to human survival, to hope and courage, to love and family. In this way Sarah's great house serves as a monument to all the pioneer women of Texas.

Kirk Sisco played the role of Charles Braches.

Anne Tremko, the actress who portrayed Matilda Lockhart.

Sarah Ashby McClure Braches' "Plum Good Soup!"

Servings: 4

2   cans plums (17 ounces each), reserve liquids
1/8   teaspoon cinnamon; dash clove
1/3   cup fresh lime juice
4   tablespoons bourbon

PREP TIME: 20 minutes.
COOK TIME: 15 minutes.

Remove pits from plums, reserving syrup and liquids from plums. Combine all ingredients in blender and blend. Pour blended soup into pot and heat over medium-low heat, stirring occasionally. Heat will evaporate alcohol from bourbon. Delicious with a garnish of sour cream that has been whisked with grated orange zest and powdered sugar. Top with mint sprig. A great and unusual appetizer for Sunday brunch company.

TESTED RECIPE
Per serving: 58 Calories 🌿 less than one gram Fat (7% calories from fat) 🌿 0g Protein
6g Carbohydrate 🌿 0mg Cholesterol 🌿 0mg Sodium

Texas Ranger Steak

"TO MAKE A MAN HAPPY"

Bartlett McClure

Servings: 4

1/4   cup extra virgin olive oil
1   tablespoon mustard pommery-style
3   tablespoons red wine
1   teaspoon Worcestershire sauce
1   teaspoon garlic powder
3   tablespoons bourbon
1 1/3 pounds sirloin steak, trimmed
     salt, pepper, and garlic powder

PREP TIME: 10 minutes plus marinating time.
COOK TIME: 8 minutes.

Make marinade with first six ingredients by whisking together. Put marinade into 9" x 13" pan and add steak, turning to coat. Marinate at room temperature for 1 hour, turning a couple of times. When ready to cook, pour off marinade and pat steak dry. Liberally season with salt, pepper and garlic powder. Heat skillet on cooktop over medium-high heat until drop of water sizzles when dropped into pan. Reduce heat to medium. Spray steak lightly with non-stick spray. Sear steak on first side and allow to cook for about 4 minutes taking care not to burn meat. Season other side of meat with salt, pepper and garlic powder, and spray with non-stick spray. Sear other side of steak and allow to cook for 3 or 4 minutes. Meat should be seared on outside and rare on inside. Remove steak and let rest for 5 to 10 minutes while deglazing pan. With pan still over heat, deglaze by pouring about 1/3 cup water into pan and scraping up browned bits from bottom of pan. Slice meat and serve with au jus gravy.

TESTED RECIPE
*Per serving: 221 Calories 🌿 9g Fat (37% calories from fat) 🌿 32g Protein 🌿 1g Carbohydrate
92mg Cholesterol 🌿 149mg Sodium * Nutritional analysis assumes only 10% of marinade is absorbed by meat.

Celebration Chicken

"FOR MARCH 2ND
TEXAS INDEPENDENCE DAY PARTY"

Charles Braches

To segment orange, cut peel and pith (orange and and white part) from fruit. Holding fruit in your hand, take a knife and slice on either side of membrane until all orange segments have been released. Set segments aside and squeeze juice from remaining part of orange into a measuring cup. Add enough fresh juice to make 3/4 cup and set aside. Lay chicken breasts on flat surface. Lightly sprinkle both sides with salt and pepper. Place prosciutto evenly on top of chicken. Fold each breast in half and secure with an uncooked piece of spaghetti. Chicken should be like a packet with prosciutto inside. Season about 1/3 cup of flour with salt and pepper. Melt butter over medium-high heat taking care not to overbrown or burn. Quickly dredge chicken packets in seasoned flour and brown on each side, about 3 minutes per side. Preheat oven to 350 degrees. Remove chicken to a 9" x 13" baking pan. Deglaze the skillet with the chicken stock, scaping up any browned bits. Bring to boil and pour liquid from skillet to baking pan with chicken. Bake chicken with broth for 25 minutes. Remove breast packets to serving platter. Place pan with juices on cooktop and add port, orange juice, jelly, orange segments, orange and lemon rinds and ginger. Stir over meduim heat. Make a slurry with sherry and cornstarch and add to skillet stirring constantly. Simmer for 10 to 15 minutes until mixture thickens to sauce consistency. Serve sauce over chicken. ❧

Chicken is delicious over Texas basmati rice that has been mixed with toasted sliced almonds and a few green onion tops. Use only the colored part of the citrus rind when grating. The white part or pith is bitter. Garnish with "rose" made from long piece of orange peel wrapped around itself. Secure base with uncooked spaghetti, add fresh basil leaves for the leaves of the rose.

Servings: 6

1	segmented orange
3/4	cup orange juice, freshly squeezed
6	boneless, skinless chicken breast halves
	salt and pepper
1/4	pound prosciutto (fat removed), or ham
	uncooked spaghetti
	flour for dredging
1/2	cup butter, melted
2	cups chicken stock (can substitute broth)
1	cup port wine
1	tablespoon currant jelly
1	grated orange rind
1	grated lemon rind
1/8	teaspoon ginger
2	tablespoons sherry
2	tablespoons cornstarch

PREP TIME BEFORE
SAUTÉING: 45 minutes.
BAKE TIME: 25 minutes.
TIME TO MAKE SAUCE:
20 minutes.

TESTED RECIPE

Per serving: 415 Calories ❧ 19g Fat (46% calories from fat) ❧ 33g Protein
15g Carbohydrate ❧ 119mg Cholesterol ❧ 999mg Sodium

Estancia de Don Jose Antonio

Navarro

"The fourth person in the room below was Euphemia's friend Juan Seguin. He called her **mijita**, my dear little daughter. She loved his kindness and the way he always seemed dressed for a ball. Sometimes she imagined herself dancing with the dark and handsome Juan Seguin. He was from an old and aristocratic family—his father, Don Erasmos, had been born in San Antonio, and the Seguin family had been respected landed gentry in the area for nearly one hundred years."

Growing up in Seguin I heard about distinguished men who had lived in the area—members of the Texas legislature, a U.S. congressman, Texas Rangers, two Generals of the Confederacy and other military leaders and war heroes. I was told about one black soldier awarded the *Croix de Guerre* by France for services during World War I, at a time when the U.S. Army awarded no medals to blacks, and I learned about a German-American pilot who earned four medals within months after the U.S. entered World War II.

None was more distinguished than José Antonio Navarro, who in the 1830's established an *estancia* near the headwaters of Geronimo Creek. Navarro's cattle, sheep and horses prospered on the prairie north of Seguin that in those days still had buffalo.

But Navarro was soon caught up in forces more powerful than a stampede of buffalo. He opposed Mexico's power-hungry President Santa Anna, who was long known to Navarro and to his friend Juan Seguin. As a young officer of the Spanish Army in San Antonio, Santa Anna hung the severed heads of opponents from the trees.

Navarro realized he had more in common politically with the settlers from the U.S. than with the dictator. In October of 1835, a Congress controlled by Santa Anna voided the Constitution, removing the last legal obstacles to his total domination of Mexico.

By the time Santa Anna marched into Texas early in 1836, Navarro was among the leaders of the Texas Revolution. While Juan Seguin carried a message from the Alamo to Colonel Fannin in Goliad, Navarro headed to Washington-on-the-Brazos. On March 2, 1836, José Antonio Navarro signed the Texas Declaration of Independence. Two weeks later, he signed the Constitution of the Republic of Texas. Only one other signer was Texas-born.

Later, after being captured in the Santa Fe expedition, Navarro

Nothing seemed changed. The Navarro sheep still grazed like clouds in the grass turning brown in the summer sun. The six Navarro children were gathered beneath the Mesquite and Osage Orange shading the patio, listening to a tutor describe in three languages the world beyond their land.

Don José Antonio Navarro

Navarro was confined to the terrible dungeons of San Juan de Ulloa. On special orders of Santa Anna, he was chained to an iron ring in the floor of his cell. Because Santa Anna considered Navarro's signing of the Texas Declaration of Independence an act of treason, he condemned Don José to death.

was imprisoned by Santa Anna. His wife, Margarita de la Garza de Navarro, wrote letters to friends and relatives in Mexico seeking his release, and eventually he returned to Texas.

When annexation was approved, Navarro served in an assembly that wrote the State Constitution. He was the only member born in Texas.

In my family we have always appreciated one liberating feature of that document crafted by Navarro and the others, a provision borrowed from Mexican and Spanish law. Our State Constitution guaranteed separate property rights for married women.

But Navarro, Seguin, and the other Tejanos who supported the Revolution were often treated badly. After hearing the impassioned plea sent by Travis from the Alamo, many Americans rushed to Texas. They arrived after the fighting ended at San Jacinto, but took an ethnic and nationalistic view of the war.

Frederick Law Olmsted wrote in *A Journey Through Texas* that the Texas natives were treated "like a conquered people ... imposed upon by the newcomers, who seized their land and property without a shadow of a claim ... from several counties they have been driven out altogether. At Austin ... twenty families were driven from their homes ... A similar occurrence at Seguin, in 1854."

Seguin histories are silent about this shameful matter. But Courthouse records say a certain newcomer "took" the brands of the Flores family. The estancia belonging to the family of Juan Seguin's wife, Maria Gertrudes Flores de Abrego, lay south of town on the Guadalupe River. That land became the newcomer's as well.

Though Navarro left his ranch on the Geronimo Creek, he never abandoned his belief in a land of liberty and justice with room for all. Until his death in 1871, he lived in San Antonio, where a newspaper paid tribute: "To none ... is Texas more indebted for her existence as a republic than to Don José Antonio Navarro who ... in his devotion to the cause of Texas independence proved in his support a tower of strength."

Since those difficult days, there has been a greater recognition of the contribution to Texas history made by the Texans born under Spanish and Mexican rule.

Today the Navarro ranch house is an archaeological site, with a historical marker dedicated ten years ago. The nearby Navarro School, with 1,000 students, is itself a larger monument to this proud name. And his 1848 house at corner of South Laredo and West Nueva Streets in San Antonio is preserved as a State Historical Park.

My hometown of Seguin is named for the Texas patriot Juan Seguin, of course. His remains were removed from Nuevo Laredo and reinterred on park land in Seguin as a Bicentennial project led by the publisher of the *Seguin Gazette*, John Taylor.

Juan Seguin's descendants and admirers meet every year at the gravesite memorial to commemorate his service to Texas. And I recall a book-signing in San Antonio, when a beautiful woman in a gorgeous mink introduced herself as a great-great granddaughter of Juan Seguin. She thanked me for the sympathetic way I depicted him in *True Women*. But she did not need to thank me; it was a true story, carefully researched.

That research took my mother and me to the Sterling Memorial Library of Yale University, which had acquired some of Seguin's papers during the Depression. It was thrilling to see the handwriting of Juan Seguin and touch the actual letters warning the Texian settlers of the bloody ruthlessness of Santa Anna. These documents had been collected by the *alcalde* (mayor) of Gonzales, Andrew Ponton, among others, during the years of the Republic. At the time, Ponton likened the events to the American Revolution. Reading the letters of Juan Seguin, I heard the echo of Paul Revere's ride three-score years before.

Santa Anna offered amnesty if Don José would renounce Texas. Navarro refused and was again chained to the cell floor.

Lopez Family Christmas Eve Salad

1	large, red apple, cored and sliced
1	large banana, sliced
1	small jicama, peeled and cut into strips (if jicama is unavailable, add 2 additional red apples)
3	large oranges, peeled and sliced
1	16 ounce can sliced pickled beets, drained (reserve liquid)
2	cups pineapple chunks (preferably fresh)
1	small head of green leaf lettuce
1 1/2	cups Monterey Jack cheese, cubed
1/2	cups roasted peanuts, chopped
1	large, fresh pomegranate (if available)

Dressing:

1/2	cup mayonnaise
2	tablespoons beet liquid
2	tablespoons lime juice
2	teaspoons sugar
1/4	teaspoon salt

Gently toss the first 6 ingredients and pour onto a shallow serving platter, which has been lined with green leaf lettuce. Top with cheese cubes and sprinkle with nuts. Pour dressing over salad.

FOR DRESSING: Combine all ingredients in a measuring cup and blend well. Pour over Christmas Eve Salad and sprinkle red pomegranate seeds on top of dressing.

Muy Amiga Slaw

"INVENTED BY MY FRIEND,
VIRGINIA SPRAGUE KEMENDO"

Shred cabbage and place in large bowl with chopped onion. In sauce pan, combine sugar, vinegar, dry mustard, salt, celery seed, and pepper. Heat to boiling, remove from heat and add oil. Pour heated mixture over chopped cabbage and refrigerate covered for several hours or overnight until well marinated, stirring several times. Serve very cold with the addition of chopped tomato and chopped cilantro for added color.

Servings: 10

2	pounds head cabbage
1/3	cup onion, finely chopped
1/2	cup sugar
1/2	cup cider vinegar
1	teaspoon dry mustard
1/4	teaspoon salt
1/2	teaspoon celery seed
1/8	teaspoon coarsely ground pepper
1/3	cup salad oil

Daddy's Jalapeño Cornbread

Combine ingredients in large bowl and stir evenly until mixed. Pour into greased 9"x 9" baking dish. Bake 25 to 30 minutes in 400 degree oven.

Servings: 8

1 1/2	cups fresh cornmeal
1/2	cup whole corn, drained
1/4	cup pickled jalapeños, chopped
3/4	cup grated longhorn cheese
1/2	cup grated onion
2	tablespoons chopped pimiento
2	teaspoons baking powder
1	cup milk
2	eggs
1/4	cup salad oil

Make Everything All Right Soup

"YOUR PAPA MADE YOU SOME TEX-MEX SOUP"
— WILTON WOODS

1	3 pound hen with 2 tablespoons poultry seasoning rubbed on skin
2	garlic cloves
1	lemon, sliced
1	large onion, chopped
1	bay leaf
1	can cream of chicken broth, undiluted
1	can green enchilada sauce
1	teaspoon chili powder
1 1/2	cups mild cheddar cheese, shredded
1 1/2	cups shredded Monterey Jack cheese
2	cups chopped avocado
1	cup chopped white onion
1	cup chopped cilantro
2	cups chopped ripe tomato

Simmer first 5 ingredients in a large pot.

Cook until meat falls from bones, about 1 1/2 - 2 hours. Remove chicken from broth. Strain broth and remove bay leaf. Discard skin and bones, chop meat and add to broth. Then add next 5 ingredients to soup base. Stir and bring to a simmer.

To serve, ladle soup into warm individual bowls. Sprinkle top with some of the last 4 ingredients over soup in each bowl. 🌿

Hint: On a cold day, use warm water to heat soup bowls.

Tex-Mex Vegetables

In a large stockpot, add chicken broth, lemon juice, olive oil, ground pepper, garlic powder and oregano. Bring to a simmer. In this order, add cauliflower, carrots, celery, zucchini, poblano, and bell pepper to simmering broth. Sprinkle vegetables with salt. Cover pot and bring back to simmer. Cook vegetables for 10 to 13 minutes or until tender when pierced with a fork. Stir vegetables in the broth mixture, and drain, reserving the broth for use in a soup. Vegetables will continue to cook even after taken from pot, so it is best to remove them while they are still crisp. While vegetables are still hot, stir in olives. Taste and adjust seasonings. Serve vegetables hot. Can be chilled and served cold.

PREP TIME: 40 minutes.
COOK TIME: 15 minutes.

Any leftovers can be used to make a southwestern stirfry with leftovers from Texas Ranger Steak. Slice the steak into thin strips. Make a sauce with leftover broth thickened with cornstarch. Add the steak and vegetables to a hot skillet and quickly stirfry. Add the sauce and stir to coat. Serve over Texas basmati rice.

Servings: 8

1 1/4	cups nonfat chicken broth
2	tablespoons lemon juice, fresh
1/3	cup extra virgin olive oil
1/2	teaspoon freshly ground black pepper, or to taste
1/4	teaspoon garlic powder, or to taste
1	teaspoon oregano, or to taste
1	medium cauliflower, cut into small florets
6	medium carrots, sliced
1	cup celery, sliced
1	pound zucchini, sliced
1	poblano pepper, seeded and sliced
1	large green bell pepper, sliced
1/2	teaspoon salt, or to taste
1	cup olives, large, pimiento stuffed, sliced

TESTED RECIPE

PER SERVING: 154 CALORIES ❧ 12G FAT (68% CALORIES FROM FAT) ❧ 2G PROTEIN
11G CARBOHYDRATE ❧ 0MG CHOLESTEROL ❧ 470MG SODIUM

Chicken Fiesta

"Colorful, delicious, everyone loves it"

Servings: 12

8 cups cooked chicken meat, diced
   salt and pepper to taste
   garlic powder to taste
1/2 cup lime juice
4 teaspoons cumin powder, or to taste
2 cups chopped cilantro
1 large chopped pickled jalapeño
2 cups chopped onion (1015 or red)
4 cups chopped tomatoes
4 avocados, chopped
10 ounces sour cream
10 ounces Monterey Jack cheese, grated

Boil two 3-pound chickens in seasoned water to cover until cooked and meat falls off the bone. Remove skin, fat and bones, and dice meat. There should be about 8 cups of diced chicken meat. (Roasted chicken meat can be substituted.) Put meat into bowl, season with salt, pepper, and garlic powder, and add lime juice. Marinate chicken for about two hours, stirring chicken periodically. Just before serving, drain remaining lime juice from chicken. Warm chicken and mix in cumin, cilantro, jalapeño, and onions. Adjust seasonings. Season tomato and avocado with salt, pepper, and garlic powder. In a trifle bowl or using the outside ring of a springform pan, closed and placed onto serving platter, layer ingredients in this order: chicken, tomatoes, avocado, sour cream, and cheese. If using a trifle bowl, bring to table for presentation and serve on individual plates with tostadas (chips). If using a springform ring, slowly release ring so ingredients stay in layers. Fan chips around circle of ingredients and bring to table for presentation.

PREP TIME: 30 minutes to chop, 15 minutes to prepare chicken to cook.
COOK TIME: 1 1/2 hours to boil chicken.
ASSEMBLY TIME: 20 minutes.

TESTED RECIPE

Per serving: 765 Calories ❧ 60g Fat (69% calories from fat) ❧ 40g Protein
21g Carbohydrate ❧ 191mg Cholesterol ❧ 510mg Sodium

Salpicon Juan Seguin

"NO MAN HAS DONE MORE TO DEFEND
THE CAUSE OF FREEDOM IN TEXAS"
— ANNIE FRANKLIN

Servings: 12

1	large brisket (8 or 9 pounds), lean
1/2	large onion, coarsely chopped
1	large carrot, coarsely chopped
1	clove garlic
1	stalk celery, coarsely chopped
	salt and pepper to taste

Combine meat with the next 5 ingredients. Wrap in tin foil, place in roasting pan and bake at 275 degrees for 3 to 4 hours, until the meat is so tender that it falls apart with the touch of a fork. When the brisket is done, remove it from the meat juices and save the juices. Puree the chili adobado in a food processor or blender until it forms a thick sauce about the consistency of ketchup. Combine meat juices with adobado sauce. When the meat is cool, pull apart with your hands until it shreds like fine threads and place in a large bowl. Add chopped onions, chopped cilantro, cheese, and chile adobado sauce. Mix well. Garnish with avocado slices and chopped tomato. ❧

2	cans chile adobado
1	large finely chopped onion
2	cups finely chopped cilantro leaves
2	pounds Monterey Jack cheese, cubed (each cube approximately the size of 1 green pea)
2	large avocados (more if you like)
6	large, ripe tomatoes, peeled and finely chopped

TESTED RECIPE

PER SERVING: 430 CALORIES ❧ 17G FAT (36% CALORIES FROM FAT) ❧ 50G PROTEIN
18G CARBOHYDRATE ❧ 141MG CHOLESTEROL ❧ 309MG SODIUM

Chicken Fandango

"Don José Antonio Navarro wanted the fandango to be particularly festive"

Servings: 4 or 5

1	3 pound fryer, cut up
2	tablespoons salad oil
1/2	cup minced green pepper
1/2	cup minced onion
1	14 oz. can tomatoes with juices
1	bay leaf
1	finely chopped garlic clove
1 1/2	teaspoon salt
1/8	teaspoon pepper
1	cup white rice, uncooked
1 1/2	cups water or chicken broth
	grated cheese for garnish

Sauté chicken in oil in Dutch oven until well browned. Add the rest of the ingredients. Simmer, covered, for about 30 minutes, or until the rice is tender. Sprinkle each serving with cheese. Makes 4 or 5 generous servings.

Staci Anderson, stunt performer and actress who portrayed Jennie Boles.

Flores Ranch Enchiladas

"Señora Flores de Seguin owned a large ranch on the Guadalupe River"

Blend first six ingredients in a blender. Put mixture in a skillet. Add bay leaf; cover and simmer 30 minutes. Remove bay leaf. Mix with green chiles in a separate skillet, heat oil. Dip tortillas in oil one at a time, heating until softened. Remove tortillas and drain on paper towels. Place tortillas on work surface and divide chicken evenly among tortillas. Roll into enchiladas. Place enchiladas in baking pan. Pour green sauce over enchiladas. Bake at 350 degrees for 15 minutes. Top with sour cream and sprinkle with cheese. Garnish with avocado slices. ❧

Servings: 12

2	cups shredded chicken
1	pint sour cream
1/2	pound mild cheddar cheese, grated
2	large avocados, cut into strips
2	7 ounce cans green chiles
1	12 ounce can tomatillos
1	small chopped onion
3	cups chicken broth
2	cloves garlic, minced
2	teaspoons salt
1	bay leaf
1/2	cup of oil, more if needed
1	dozen corn tortillas

Flan Navarro

Servings: 10

1/2	*cup sugar*
14	*ounces sweetened*
	condensed milk
12	*ounces evaporated milk*
3	*eggs, well beaten*
1	*teaspoon vanilla*

Preheat oven to 375 degrees. Lightly spray loaf pan with non-stick cooking spray. Put several cups of water in pot or tea kettle and boil. Turn off heat and begin to prepare caramel.

FOR CARAMEL: Do not stir during this process. Put sugar into heavy saucepan over high heat. Sugar will begin to melt and turn brown. Swirl pan with melted sugar and watch carefully to make sure it does not burn. When sugar reaches desired color (about 6 or 7 minutes) pour into prepared pan.

FOR CUSTARD: Mix next 4 ingredients well. Pour into prepared pan on top of caramel. Place 9" x 13" pan on rack in preheated oven. Set loaf pan with flan in middle of 9" x 13" pan. Pour boiling water into 9" x 13" pan until water is about 2 inches high around loaf pan. Careful not to get water into flan! Cook flan for 50 to 60 minutes or until knife inserted in center comes out clean. Remove flan from oven, and allow to cool for about 30 minutes. Cover flan with serving platter and then invert flan onto platter, pouring any remaining syrup over dessert. Chill at least 4 hours or overnight.

TESTED RECIPE

PER SERVING: 231 CALORIES ❧ 7G FAT (28% CALORIES FROM FAT) ❧ 7G PROTEIN
35G CARBOHYDRATE ❧ 78MG CHOLESTEROL ❧ 103MG SODIUM

Mama's Pecan Pralines

Prepare area to pour pralines. Clear off table surface and lay newspaper down. Top newspaper with sheets of wax paper. Next to cooktop, have three small cups with cool water in each. Put sugars, milk, vanilla and salt in saucepan over medium heat. When sugar is almost all melted, add butter. Stir constantly and bring to a boil. This can take up to 20 minutes. Mixture will start off cloudy looking, but will turn to a clear syrup. Boil, stirring constantly for 4 minutes. Drop a few drops of syrup into one of the cups with water. If mixture breaks up when it hits the water, the pralines need to cook longer. Keep boiling, stirring and testing every 3 minutes.

Candy is ready for pecans when drops of syrup put into water hold their shape, like soft beads. This is commonly known as the soft ball stage. Candy will have thickened somewhat. Add pecans and take off heat, still stirring constantly for 2 or 3 minutes. Mixture will start to get much more syrupy. Begin pouring pralines onto wax paper in spoonfuls so that each praline is about 2 to 3 inches in diameter and contains a few pecan halves. Try to evenly distribute the pecans among all the pralines. Work quickly or the candy will harden in the pot.

CAREFUL: Praline syrup can blister skin. Allow at least 20 minutes for candy to set. Better to wait until they are completely cooled before peeling off wax paper. Wrap individual cooled pralines in plastic wrap and store in airtight tin.

Servings: 50

2	*cups sugar*
1	*cup brown sugar, packed*
1	*cup evaporated milk (8 ounces)*
1	*teaspoon vanilla*
4	*tablespoons butter*
	pinch salt
3	*cups pecan halves*

PREP TIME: 25 minutes.
COOK TIME: 40 minutes.
POUR TIME: 15 minutes.
COOL TIME: 25 minutes.

When pralines get stale, they turn from shiny and clear to cloudy and grainy. They can still be eaten, but are not at their best. Crumble and serve mixed into softened vanilla ice cream!

TESTED RECIPE

PER SERVING: 82 CALORIES ❦ 3G FAT (36% CALORIES FROM FAT) ❦ 0G PROTEIN
13G CARBOHYDRATE ❦ 3MG CHOLESTEROL ❦ 14MG SODIUM

Euphemia's New House

"'In the old days,' Euphemia Texas observed, 'when Seguin was a kind of oasis in the wilderness, it was easier to forgive or overlook the wrong people do. When you're trying to survive, you just don't have time to observe such niceties as justice and truth. But now, the more civilized we become, the less patience I have with injustice and ignorance and fools.'"

f or me, that rambling house beside the springs of King Branch was a place of inexhaustible enchantment and mystery. Sometimes our parents would allow me and my brother and some visiting cousins to go exploring and to play in the springs.

Even as a child I recognized the great natural beauty of the place. A gully that drained runoff from the gently sloping streets and fields to the north cut deeper and deeper into a little hollow, until its steep walls began to glisten and drip with spring water. Great oaks had taken root on the walls of the gully behind the house. They spread a multilayered canopy above the springs and made a home for a hundred birds that marked our movements with calls of greeting and alarm. The bottom of the gully, here deeply shaded and gently dampened, was lush with delicate ferns, tangled vines, and other vegetation completely unlike the plants in the sunbaked fields above. A trickling stream of clear waters formed and began to flow across stretches of mud and gravel, here miniature rapids, there a tiny pool, never more than a yard wide or a foot deep—but home to crawfish and other watery creatures more fascinating and more fun than any doll or toy could ever be.

King Branch moved on toward the bottoms where it joined the Guadalupe River, just a bit farther south. But our way was blocked by the great earthen bridge that carried four wide lanes of Court

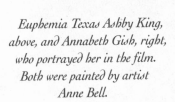

Euphemia Texas Ashby King, above, and Annabeth Gish, right, who portrayed her in the film. Both were painted by artist Anne Bell.

Street some 15 feet above the narrow brick culvert. That tunnel was so dark, so slimy, so obviously dangerous that no one I knew ever answered the standard "Dare you!" to crawl through to the other side.

Did I say dangerous? Now, as a mother and a grandmother, I draw a breath thinking back to when we played there as children. Could there have been snakes? Of course. Poison Ivy? Inevitably. Varmints, bugs, and mosquitoes? Certainly. But in fact, my parents had warned us well to watch for snakes and taught us to recognize poison ivy too. And if you live in Texas, you have to learn to cope with varmints, bugs and mosquitoes.

The worst calamity I can recall in that enchanted play place was when my little brother tried to catch a crawfish, and the lobster's little cousin caught him first, tightly fastening its tiny claw onto a tender piece of fingertip. The vicious crustacean drew blood, and tears. My brother headed home—but turned around before he made it out of the gully to play some more in the soothing waters. To us, the springs of King Branch were the most beautiful, the most wonderful place in all Seguin.

I am sure that my great-great-grandmother Euphemia and her husband William King loved the place even more than we did. They placed their log cabin beside the beautiful springs of King Branch after they were married in the town's first church in 1850, not long after Seguin had been founded by a group of Texas Rangers, including William's older brothers. The log cabin grew as their family grew—here were born their son, Henry, and their daughter, Ann—and over the years some lean-to rooms were added. Then in 1887 they hired Mr. W.H. Kishbaugh, who had married into the family, to build a new house for them. That was the same year that "Mr. Henry" built his home nearby for his bride, Bettie. Euphemia

Portrait of William G. King, painted by his daughter, Annie.

Matthew Glave, who played William in the film.

and William lived out their days in the "new" house. By the time my mother was a little girl spending the summers with her grandma, Bettie, and grandpa, "Mr. Henry," it was the home of Mr. Henry's sister Annie, known to my mother and several generations of relatives as Aunt Annie.

During the years that Aunt Annie King Colville lived here, the house grew and grew. When a side street was put in off Court Street, it gained a new front entrance and a gingerbread porch to face the street, soon shaded by a magnolia tree that lived for three-score years and ten. The house acquired new rooms for entertaining, for sleeping and for

painting; most of them surrounding a courtyard or patio that opened to the south. On that side, the yard sloped away, carrying a path down to a rustic footbridge across a draw to Court Street. Scarlet amaryllis marked the terraces that stepped down to the little bridge, and a Seven Sisters rose climbed across it. After a rainstorm, runoff from a field of wildflowers—I most remember the gorgeous gaillardia—went down the draw to King Branch.

With the help of sharecroppers, Aunt Annie farmed the land she had inherited until the barn and sheds that stood north of the house were

Euphemia's sons return from the Wild Horse Roundup.

destroyed by an arsonist. Then in her last years she rented out the land for others to work.

In many ways Aunt Annie's life fulfilled the dream of her mother's generation. Like her Aunt Sarah Ashby McClure Braches and her mother Euphemia, Annie was educated. Unlike them however, she was able to enjoy a life of cultured refinement. They came to Texas talking of taming the frontier and bringing civilization to the wilderness. To do that they rode horseback, plowed fields, escaped from wild animals, and fought Mexican armies and Indian raiding parties—so their children could live better.

Aunt Annie lived the better life they had in mind. She was an artist, a painter, and she liked to set up her easel in a well-lit room off the courtyard, or in the courtyard itself. When she was growing up, my mother visited her regularly and often found her painting. When I was growing up, I remember visiting my own aunts, cousins, and family friends, and being shown the paintings they had received from Aunt Annie.

But Annie was Euphemia's daughter, and she never forgot where she came from or the sacrifices made to get her to a fine home in a sophisticated small town. When her parents moved into "Euphemia's new house," they kept the log cabin that had been their home for almost 40 years. They peeled away the later lean-to additions, but proudly kept the original cabin in its place above the springs of King Branch. After her parents passed on, Aunt Annie kept the cabin as well, using it in a small way to store garden tools, and in a larger way as a prompt or a prop for her stories. She liked to tell about Euphemia, who had lived there, and about her other female forebears.

In 1936, despite the hard times of the Depression, all of Texas was caught up in celebrating its Centennial. Of course, back then the population included many like Annie—daughters and sons, and grandsons and granddaughters, who had actually known the men and women of the Revolution and the Runaway Scrape and the days of the Republic of Texas. For them the oral history was first-hand and fresh, and the passions were strong.

That year, Annie was asked to lend the log cabin of her parents for a display in Fort Worth of the Texas Rangers for the Texas Centennial. She proudly agreed. Her father, like his brothers and like most of the men in early Seguin, had served as a Ranger, as needed, for many years. The family's proud relic was carefully measured and each log marked before it was disassembled and transported to Fort Worth.

That year, too, my mother was a young woman soon to be married. Full of thoughts about her family and the future, she visited her Aunt Annie to share the news of her wedding plans. My mother found the old woman surrounded by potted ferns and elephant ears on the shaded patio of her house and, despite her apparent illness, she was busily working on a painting she called "The Road from the Alamo."

Many years later my mother passed along the lessons of its symbolism as explained by Aunt Annie. In the background was the Alamo, where Texans fought and died for liberty. Then through an open field of bluebonnets in the center she put a road leading to a row of flags in the foreground because, as she said, her family's history stretched right through the center of Texas history, from the Revolution and the years of the Republic, through the Confederacy, and finally to statehood in the United States. Annie reminded my mother that she could follow the

Annie King Colville holds her degree from Baylor College for Women.

history of the women in her family along the road that passed right
outside her house.

That day Aunt Annie talked about that road, and about the women
whose lives spent along that road were so much a part of Texas history.
The road from the Alamo began in San Antonio some 35 miles to the
west of Seguin. It passed Annie's own home, built for her mother
Euphemia beside the beautiful springs of King Branch. That same road
passed the house just up the hill that Annie's brother, Henry, had built
for his wife, Bettie. It continued out Capote Road and by the farm
where Bettie grew up. The road kept going to Gonzales, the Cradle of
Texas Liberty, and another eight miles beyond to Peach Creek, where
the great house of Sarah McClure Braches still stood. Under the oaks
there, Sam Houston had gathered his soldiers to begin their long retreat;
there Euphemia and her sister Sarah and the Widows of the Alamo
began the Runaway Scrape. They all fled before the advancing army of

Annie's painting "The Road from the Alamo"

Santa Anna, until the road ended at San Jacinto and Texas was free.

That was the last time my mother saw her great-aunt Annie. The Centennial year that should have been one of celebration was instead a tragic one for her family. Within little more than a year, Annie's grandson Lynch Colville was killed in a shooting accident in the bottoms of the Guadalupe River, Aunt Annie died and both her sons, Myron Colville and William King Colville, died as well, of natural causes.

Amid the compounding grief, no one followed up when the log cabin built by William and Euphemia failed to return as promised from the Texas Rangers exhibition in Fort Worth. Sadly, as many times as I have heard this story told, by many different members of the family, I never heard of anyone who thought that the century-old log cabin was simply lost.

For many years my mother treasured Aunt Annie's stories about the family history, and she treasured the painting Annie was finishing on that day. Later my mother gave me Aunt Annie's painting of "The Road from the Alamo." I have kept it near me; today the painting hangs on my office wall. The stories about Annie's mother, Euphemia, and her aunt Sarah McClure Braches, and even some tales she told about her sister-in-law Bettie King, had long been a part of the family stories that my mother passed on to me. I treasured them as well, and kept them close to my heart, and then I put them in *True Women*.

William, Euphemia, and their dog, Peaches

Lucinda Saphronia Miller's Juneteenth Salad

"MADE ESPECIALLY FOR ABRAHAM LINCOLN MILLER"

Servings: 6

6	large potatoes
2	tablespoons vinegar
5	tablespoons salad oil
1/4	teaspoon dry mustard
1/4	teaspoon paprika
1	teaspoon celery salt
2	teaspoons salt
1/2	cup mayonnaise
1	tablespoon prepared mustard
1	cup sour cream
4	hard-cooked eggs, chopped
1	large onion, finely chopped
1 1/2	cups olives, sliced
1 1/2	cups garlic dill pickles, coarsely chopped
1	cup diced celery
3	tablespoons caraway seeds red and green pepper rings, for garnish

Boil potatoes in their jackets until tender when pierced with a knife. Cool, peel, and cut into chunks. In a separate bowl, mix vinegar, salad oil, dry mustard, paprika, and celery salt. Salt potatoes. Pour mixture over potatoes. Stir in mayonnaise, prepared mustard, and sour cream. Add eggs, onions, olives, chopped dill pickles, and celery, and gently fold with spoon. Add caraway seeds and stir. Decorate with red and green pepper rings, if you wish. ❧

TESTED RECIPE

Rowdy King Boys' Chile Con Queso

"COOKED IN AN IRON SKILLET OVER AN OPEN FIRE ON THE WILD HORSE ROUNDUP"

In heavy skillet, melt butter and sauté onion until translucent and tender. Add chiles, tomatoes and their juices. Stir until well heated. Add cheese and allow it to melt. Stir to incorporate ingredients. Serve warm with tortilla chips. Delicious over broiled, boneless chicken breast served over rice. Garnish with cilantro leaves. If using Velveeta, this may be frozen.

Servings: 10

1	large onion, chopped
4	cups Monterey Jack cheese (or Velveeta), cubed
14	ounces chopped green chiles (2 - 7 ounce cans)
14 1/2	ounces canned tomatoes, chopped with juices
2	sticks of butter

PREP TIME:
25 minutes.

COOK TIME:
20 minutes.

William and John King

TESTED RECIPE

PER SERVING: 210 CALORIES ❧ 16G FAT (67% CALORIES FROM FAT) ❧ 12G PROTEIN
5G CARBOHYDRATE ❧ 46MG CHOLESTEROL ❧ 392MG SODIUM

Euphemia's Favorite Cake, 1880

Servings: 24

1	*pound sugar (about 2 cups)*
1	*pound butter (4 sticks), room temperature*
1	*tablespoon orange juice, freshly squeezed*
1	*tablespoon grated lemon rind*
1	*pound flour (about 3 1/4 cups)*
1	*tablespoon baking powder*
16	*egg whites* (divided into batches)*

Preheat oven to 325 degrees. Butter bundt pan. Cream sugar and butter. Add juice and rind. Gradually add flour and baking powder. Beat egg whites in two batches of eight whites each until stiff peaks form. Lighten batter by stirring in a half of one of the batches of beaten whites (approximately 4 beaten whites). Then as gently as possible, fold in the rest of the beaten whites in four or five batches. Pour batter into prepared pan and tap pan on countertop so that any trapped air pockets will rise to the top of the cake. Bake for 1 hour and 10 minutes or until toothpick inserted into center of cake comes out dry. Let cake cool in pan for about 30 minutes to 1 hour before inverting.

PREP TIME: 1 hour.
COOK TIME: 1 hour 10 minutes.

*   Can use reconstituted pasteurized dried egg whites

TESTED RECIPE

PER SERVING: 289 CALORIES ❦ 16G FAT (48% CALORIES FROM FAT) ❦ 4G PROTEIN
34G CARBOHYDRATES ❦ 41MG CHOLESTEROL ❦ 239MG SODIUM

Aunt Annie's Gingerbread and Hardsauce

Preheat oven to 350 degrees. Lightly grease and flour 9" x 9" baking pan. In a medium bowl, mix together dry ingredients, except sugar. In a separate bowl, heat oil and sugar on high until well blended. Add eggs, one at a time, beating well after each addition. Sift one-half of dry ingredients into oil mixture. Mix at medium speed until blended, stopping once to scrape bottom and sides of bowl. Add applesauce, vanilla, water and molasses to batter and mix until combined. Sift in remaining dry ingredients and mix until just blended. Do not overheat. Pour into prepared pan and bake until toothpick inserted into center comes out clean, about 40 minutes. Serve with Hardsauce. ❧

PREP TIME: 25 minutes.
BAKE TIME: 40 minutes.

THE HARDSAUCE: Separate egg. Have water simmering in bottom of double boiler. In top of double boiler but not over heat, cream butter and sugar. Now assemble double boiler and add egg yolk to sugar mixture, beating constantly. Blend in lemon rind and brandy. In another bowl, beat egg white until stiff peaks form. Fold into mixture in double boiler and cook, gently stirring, until sauce is very warm. Serve warm over gingerbread or bread pudding, about 3 tablespoons per serving. ❧

For a different twist, pour Vanilla Sauce from Hawkins Plantation Cake on plate and make a design with Caramel Sauce. Then top with gingerbread square.

PREP TIME: 15 minutes.
COOK TIME: 15 minutes.

Servings: 12

Gingerbread:

1/4	cup canola oil
1/3	cup unsweetened applesauce
1	cup sugar, superfine if available
2/3	cup molasses
2	large eggs
1/3	cup water
2	teaspoons vanilla
2	cups all-purpose flour
3	teaspoons ground ginger
2	teaspoons ground cinnamon
1 1/2	teaspoons baking soda
1	teaspoon ground cloves
1	teaspoon ground allspice
1/2	teaspoon salt

Hardsauce:

1/2	cup butter, very soft, at room temperature
1 1/2	cups sifted powdered sugar
1	egg, separated
3	tablespoons brandy or cognac
1	teaspoon grated lemon rind

TESTED RECIPE

Georgia's
Mansion on th

Hill

"When Georgia looked up from her vegetables, the sun was behind the Yankee lieutenant and she couldn't see his features. She was not sure how to greet one's former enemy. She stood and held out her hand. He ignored the gesture. 'It's my duty to inform you this house has been designated headquarters for the officers and men who will occupy this town.'"

The story of my great grandparents, Georgia and Peter C. Woods, I learned from my father, Wilton Woods.

Daddy was an avid student of the Civil War events pertaining to the lives of Georgia and Peter Woods.

Julie Carmen played Cherokee Hawkins Lawshe

Michael York played Capt. Lewis Lawshe

Peter C. Woods was born in Shelbyville, Tennessee, December 30, 1819. Upon graduation from the Louisville Kentucky Medical Institute in 1842, he met and married Georgia Virginia Lawshe, a granddaughter of Benjamin Hawkins, member of the Continental Congress, and one of the first two Senators from North Carolina to take a seat in the United States Senate in January 1790.

In 1850, Dr. Woods and family moved from Water Valley, Mississippi, to Bastrop, Texas, and on to San Marcos in 1853. While he practiced medicine, his wife Georgia assumed the responsibility of managing the 4,000 acre plantation and the slaves, while bearing seven children.

In the late fall of 1861 and the first few weeks of 1862, Dr. Woods recruited, and became captain of, the 32nd Texas Cavalry, taking the oath of allegiance to the Confederate States of America on February 22, 1862. When the regiment was organized, he was elected colonel and commanded the unit throughout the war in the Rio Grande Valley, along the Texas coast, and in the Red River Campaign. The Woods regiment participated in all of the battles of the Red River Campaign from Pleasant Hill, Louisiana, April 8, 1864, to the final battle described as "a stand-up, no-quarter, fire fight along Yellow Bayou," where Colonel Doctor Woods was severely wounded, May 18, 1864.

After the Civil War, he returned to the plantation at San Marcos and to the practice of medicine. During the war years, Georgia Woods managed the plantation and raised cotton which she shipped by wagon trains to Mexico to be sold by running the blockade as long as that market lasted. Dr. Woods served in the Texas Constitutional Convention of 1866. In 1872, Georgia Lawshe Woods died at age 41. The colonel doctor died January 27, 1898.

by Wilton G. Woods

*Wedding Portraits of Cherokee Hawkins
and Capt. Lewis Lawshe*

Georgia's parents were married
August 10, 1819 at Ft. Hawkins, now
Macon, Georgia. Their daughter,
Georgia Virginia Lawshe, was born
at the Hawkins Plantation on
January 31, 1831.

Hawkins Plantation

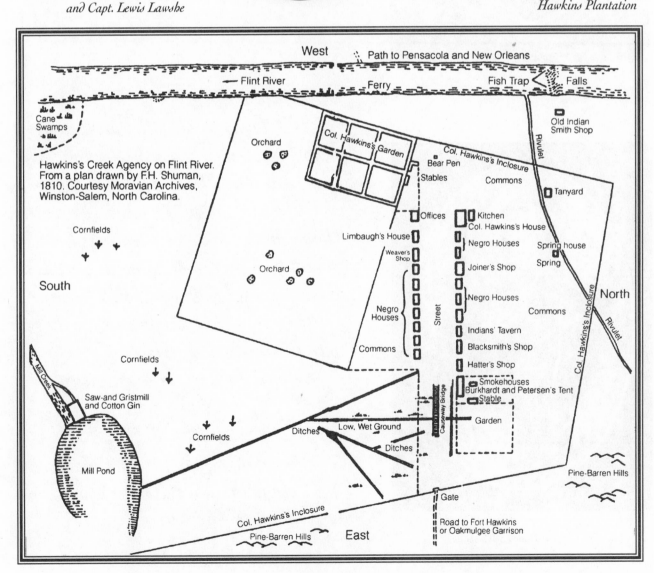

West   Path to Pensacola and New Orleans

Flint River   Ferry   Fish Trap   Falls

Cane
Swamps

Old Indian
Smith Shop

Orchard

Col. Hawkins's Garden

Col. Hawkins's Inclosure

Rivulet

Hawkins's Creek Agency on Flint River.
From a plan drawn by F.H. Shuman,
1810. Courtesy Moravian Archives,
Winston-Salem, North Carolina.

Bear Pen

Stables   Commons

Tanyard

Offices   Kitchen
Col. Hawkins's House

Cornfields

Limbaugh's House   Negro Houses   Spring house

Weaver's
Shop   Joiner's Shop   Spring

South   Orchard

Negro Houses

Negro
Houses   Street   Commons   North

Rivulet

Commons   Indians' Tavern
Blacksmith's Shop

Hatter's Shop

Col. Hawkins's Inclosure

Cornfields   Smokehouses
Burkhardt and Petersen's Tent
Stable

Mill Creek

Saw-and Gristmill
and Cotton Gin   Causeway Bridge   Garden

Cornfields   Low, Wet Ground

Ditches   Ditches

Pine-Barren Hills

Mill Pond

Gate

Col. Hawkins's Inclosure

Pine-Barren Hills   East   Road to Fort Hawkins
or Oakmulgee Garrison

83

Georgia Virginia Lawshe Woods

Civil War letters of Georgia and Col. Dr. Peter C. Woods– 1862–1864

EXCERPTS TAKEN FROM A COLLECTION OF SIXTY LETTERS.

Col. Dr. Peter C. Woods

Dear Doctor Peter,

This leaves us all well, but very lonely. Home was never so lonely. Last spring when you first left us, I lived in the garden and took a great deal of active exercise. Now I have sewing to do, preparation for Methodist Conference, not so much outdoors work. Sometimes I feel as though I could hardly live here anymore, but I will not trouble you with unnecessary complaining.

Good night – As ever your devoted wife,

G. V. Woods

October 25, 1862

Lovie thinks if you get home and we have peace again, that she will never again have to be afraid of burglars.

Dear Doctor Peter,

I shall never get used to your being away from home. You are missed so much. I have to start around to keep off the blues. I rise early to get time for secret devotions.

I hardly know how to address a letter to you. It does not come natural for me to say anything but Doc. Peter. You must excuse me.

Affectionately, G.V. Woods

When he spoke of Georgia, Daddy called her by her maiden name, Georgia Lawshe, and with obvious admiration he used her life story as a role model for us. Daddy loved and respected Dr. Woods as a gentle physician, a public leader, and a superb horseman.

My dear wife,

Word of our child is like a spring day in the middle of winter. I heartily rejoice and thank God for the life He is entrusting to our care. How I love you and wish I could be at your side. Try to preserve your health as well as you can. I fear you have too much to do for your constitution. I would enjoy a visit home so much. I am exceedingly wearied of the war. What outcome could possibly be worth all this desolation and death? How much more valuable I would be to the Creator if I were at your side as you give life to the world and not what I have been so recently asked to give.

Your husband, P.C. Woods

My Dear Husband,
    I need your counsel and your advice very often.
                                Affectionately,
                                G. V. Woods ~ May 23, 1862

Dear Doctor Peter,
    I am trying to manage home affairs as best I can. Your horses are beginning to fall off and scatter. I don't know whether it would be best to take them to the ranch or not. Sol has gone to Col. Ellison's to make his Negroes' shoes. I rather think I will not commence sowing grass until Sol gets home and it will take a little time to get the cotton out. I do hope we have a good crop season.
                                G. V. Woods
                                October 27, 1863

Dear Doctor Peter,
    You are as dearly beloved and as much missed as you were when you first left home. I cannot get used to living without you. I hope and trust I may never have that lesson to learn.
                                Affectionately, G. V. Woods
                                November 24, 1863

Dear Doctor Peter,

I got the seed corn off Mr. Garth and had a bushel of potatoes from Mr. Bolls. The hands are sowing wheat and for a rarity it rained so hard that the ground was too wet to plant the first part of this week. I am going to try very hard to make no debts. Brother McKie wants all the grass seed that I can spare for him. I don't know what to price them. As ever your devoted wife—

G. V. Woods   February 12, 1863

Martha Benjamin Hawkins Lawshe

Dear Doctor Peter,

The weather has been so cold for some days, we could do nothing but go and get wood to make fires and sit by them. One side would fry when the other was freezing. We are having trouble with worms in the colts. Leroy had the black horses driven up. Since dinner I went down to see him doctor the two little colts. We are trying a medicine of tea or coffee, whiskey and tobacco made very strong. Leroy says it makes the worms drunk and he can get them out. G. V. Woods—January 9, 1864

Martha Benjamin Hawkins Lawshe, daughter of Madison Hawkins and Mahalia, a slave woman. Martha Benny was first cousin of Georgia.

My Dear Wife,
     Be sure to attend to the small pox vaccinations of all hands black and white. God bless my wife and little ones.
                                        P. C. Woods
                                        January 18, 1862

My Darling Georgia,
     There is nothing at present that so much relieves me in the many cares from which I am daily surrounded as the news I occasionally receive from home.   Your devoted husband,
                                        P. C. Woods
                                        June 15, 1862

Dear Doctor Peter,
     I have tried to keep you appraised of our acts and our doings. I am having wheat sowed now and I will try to get ready to plant corn by the first day of February if the weather continues to be springlike. We've had a very little rain this winter and if we don't plant early, I fear that we won't make crops or corn.

                    As ever your devoted wife,
                    G. V. Woods   January 24, 1864

Dear Doctor Peter,

Miss Mollie Caldwell spent a day with us. I was so very busy with the outdoor work. She said she thought you would _set me free_ when you got home. I told her if you did not, I would set myself free. If we are ever permitted to live at peace in our home again, you may expect to take back on all of the outdoor business — back into your own hands, but I think I shall forevermore feel more interested in any and everything that concerns you.

Affectionately, G.V. Woods

November 21, 1863

Dear Doctor Peter,

You did not say whether your new horse had gotten into camp or not. I would like so much to know if you were pleased at my sending him. Did the hat fit? And did you need it? You were needing a hat very much when I last saw you.

Your loved one, G.V. Woods

October 27, 1863

My Dear Wife,

I have had a very bad cold for some days but not at all sick. I think I will be over it in a day or two. All of this comes from not having a warm bed companion. I frequently think of you—especially at certain times. I know of nothing that I do so desire as to spend my Christmas at home with you, but it won't do for me to think too much about that sacred pleasuring that is only known to you and to myself.

As ever your devoted husband,
P. C. Woods
November 26, 1863

Dear Doctor Peter,

I love you very dearly, but that is not news to you, only that I felt like writing it. All hands are in bed but me and I feel like I can't just keep on writing. I believe we will always have strength sufficient for our every trial.

G. V. Woods
December 13, 1863

My Darling Georgia,

I shall be 45 years old at which age every man should be permitted to retire to private life, especially when it is a boon greatly desired. If I should not get home soon, you must take care of yourself as I expect many days of pleasure with you even in our old age.

Your husband, P.C. Woods
February 17, 1864

Dear Doctor Peter,

You know it has not been my disposition to make a great ado about anything, but that is no sign that I don't feely as deeply as anyone. I think that I love more devotedly than most other persons. My love of my husband comes next to my love of my God. Sometimes I fear it is the first. Next is the love for my children.

Devotedly, G.V. Woods
January 24, 1864

My Dear Wife,

Oh, how I wish I could be with you if only for a short time. How pleasant to contemplate. Be sure to write me often, if only you give but a few lines. I still write any and every chance I get.

Farewell, P.C. Woods
October 6, 1863

Jeff Nordling played Col. Dr. Peter C. Woods

My Darling Georgia,

We were riding along a sandbar in the river when we saw a Federal gunboat hard aground in the sand. General Tom Green ordered the men to take the vessel and charge into the concentrated fire of the enemy. He had been drinking hard and I knew what he ordered was suicide. I knew it was a trap. It would be foolhardy and lead us to useless slaughter and I refused to order the assault. Our horses were under direct enemy fire. He was yelling at us to charge when he was struck down by a Yankee gunner. I will ever wonder if Tom Green, one of the greatest soldiers Texas ever produced, would be alive if I had obeyed his order. But I am comforted by the fact many more of my own men are living. Do I have the right to judge who should live and who should die?

   Farewell dear wife –
   P. C. Woods
   April 10, 1864

Oriana Huron played Cherokee Woods

Tony Todd played Ed Tom Lawshe

My Dear Wife,
    I expected a letter from you by last mail but I was disappointed. There seems to be some irregularity in our mail facilities at present. In fact everything connected with the government is in a lamentable, demoralized condition. I am at a loss to know where we are to land. We are now out on the great sea of uncertainty without direction. I have begun to fear the anchor may be lost. If so, and we are turned loose amid the breakers – if so, our destruction is sure. Still, I live in hope.   God keep you.
                                        P. C. Woods
                                    February 21, 1864

Darling Doctor Peter,
    I would not have you give up your position as soldier to be with me. I will suffer and endure until death rather than be subject to the Yankees. Remember that your life is in the hands of an all-mercifull Heavenly Father who can and will take care of you. He will bring you home in peace and safety some day in His own good time.

                    G. V. Woods
                May 5, 1864

Queen of Tuckabatchee Corn Pudding

"NAME OF A MYTHICAL GRANDMOTHER"

Servings: 8

1/4	cup butter
1/4	cup flour
2	teaspoons salt
1 1/2	tablespoons sugar
1 3/4	cups half and half, warmed
3	cups corn, fresh or frozen
3	eggs

Butter a casserole dish and preheat oven to 350 degrees. Melt butter in a saucepan over medium heat. Whisk in flour, salt and sugar. Cook about 4 minutes, whisking constantly. Do not let mixture brown. Add in warmed half and half, stirring constantly. Continue to cook and stir until thick. Remove from heat. Stir in corn. Beat eggs in a separate bowl until frothy. Slowly add eggs while stirring. Pour into prepared pan and bake in a hot water bath for 45 minutes or until center of pudding is slightly "jiggly" but not liquid. Serve hot. 🌿

PREP TIME: 25 minutes. BAKE TIME: 45 minutes.

This dish can be used as a vegetable to accompany baked turkey or ham, or as a dessert topped with molasses.

TESTED RECIPE

Per Serving: 216 Calories 🌿 14g Fat (56% calories from fat) 🌿 6g Protein
19g Carbohydrate 🌿 103mg Cholesterol 🌿 641mg Sodium

Aunt Sweet's Methodist Ladies Cookies

"NAMED ALL HER SONS FOR METHODIST BISHOPS"

Servings: 36

1	egg white
1	cup brown sugar
1	tablespoon flour
1/4	teaspoon salt
1	cup pecans, chopped

Preheat oven to 325 degrees. In a mixing bowl, beat egg white until stiff. Add brown sugar and beat on high until thoroughly incorporated. Add flour and salt, and mix until dry ingredients are incorporated. Stir in pecans. Grease cookie sheet. Drop batter by small teaspoonfuls onto prepared cookie sheet, spacing cookies about 2 inches apart. Bake for 10 minutes. Allow cookies to partly cook on sheet before removing to a cooling rack. Store cooled cookies in an airtight container. 🌿

PREP TIME: 15 minutes.

BAKE TIME: 10 minutes.

TESTED RECIPE

Per Serving: 27 Calories 🌿 1g Fat (34% calories from fat) 🌿 0g Protein
4g Carbohydrate 🌿 0mg Cholesterol 🌿 18mg Sodium

The Reverend Andrew Jackson Potter's Hellfire and Brimstone Chili

"MY HEART WAS TOUCHED BY THE COLD IRON OF THE SACRED TRUTH"

In a small bowl, make seasoning mix by mixing together chili con carne spice, cumin, paprika, red pepper flakes, cayenne pepper, salt and black pepper. In a large pot, brown pork sausage over medium high heat. Drain off fat. Add beef and some of seasoning mix. Stir and brown meat. When browned, add onion and some more of seasoning mix. Stir and cook until onions are translucent. Add remaining ingredients, including rest of seasoning mix, except one bottle of beer, cilantro, jalapeño, sour cream and cheese. Cook chili over low heat for about 3 hours, stirring occasionally, and adding the other bottle of beer as needed. When chili reaches completion, meat will break up when mixture is stirred. To serve, ladle 1 1/2 cups into a bowl. Top with 1/2 ounce grated cheese, 1 tablespoon sour cream, some of the chopped cilantro and some of the yellow jalapeño.

Makes a festive looking main course that packs a powerful punch. Serve with a salad and Daddy's Jalapeño Cornbread for a wonderful winter meal. Freezes well.

PREP TIME: 45 minutes.
COOK TIME: 3 hours.

Servings: 24

6	tablespoons chili con carne spice
2 1/2	tablespoons cumin
1	tablespoon paprika
2	teaspoons red pepper flakes
2	teaspoons cayenne
2	tablespoons salt
3	teaspoons pepper, coarsely ground
1	pound pork sausage
9	pounds chopped chuck roast, or beef stew meat
2	medium onions, chopped
2	cups tomatoes, chopped
1	cup canned tomato puree
5	cloves garlic, chopped
2	teaspoons fine herbs
24	ounces dark Mexican beer (2 bottles)
1/2	cup cilantro, finely chopped, divided
2	medium yellow jalapeños finely chopped, divided
24	tablespoons sour cream
12	ounces grated Monterey Jack cheese, divided

Reverend Andrew Jackson Potter

TESTED RECIPE
PER SERVING: 546 CALORIES ❦ 42G FAT (70% CALORIES FROM FAT) ❦ 34G PROTEIN
6G CARBOHYDRATE ❦ 130MG CHOLESTEROL ❦ 882MG SODIUM

Hawkins Plantation Cake

"FOR MR. BENJAMIN"

Servings: 24

Cake:

2	sticks butter, room temperature
2	cups sugar
5	eggs
2	cups cake flour, sifted
2	teaspoons vanilla
1/2	teaspoon lemon juice
1/4	teaspoon salt
1	cup peach preserves

Cream Sauce:

3	cups whipping cream
3	tablespoons sugar
2	teaspoons vanilla

Caramel Sauce:

1/2	cup sugar
3/4	cup whipping cream
1	tablespoon butter
1	tablespoon honey

FOR CAKE: Preheat oven to 325 degrees. Grease bundt pan very lightly with less than 1 teaspoon of butter. In a large mixing bowl, cream sugar and butter. Beat in whole eggs one at a time. Sift 2 cups cake flour into mixture and mix. Add vanilla, lemon juice and salt, and mix. Pour into prepared pan. Tap pan or hard surface to force any bubbles in batter to rise to the top. Bake for 50 minutes or until toothpick inserted into cake comes out clean. Allow cake to cool in pan for about 10 minutes before inverting onto a serving platter.

Angelina Jolie, as painted by Anne Bell, portrayed Georgia in the film.

FOR CREAM SAUCE: Put all ingredients into heavy saucepan over low heat until sauce is reduced by one-half, and thickens somewhat. Stir occasionally. This takes as long as 15 minutes. Strain mixture into container and chill. Sauce will thicken as it cools.

FOR CARAMEL SAUCE: In a saucepan, brown sugar in butter over medium heat until it is caramel in color, about 5 to 10 minutes. Warm cream in separate saucepan. Carefully add warmed cream to caramel, stirring constantly. Add honey and stir. Keep stirring caramel sauce until all ingredients are melted and blended, and sauce is thickened, about 10 more minutes.

TO ASSEMBLE: Slice cake horizontally into 2 layers. Spread peach preserves over bottom layer and replace top layer. Slice cake into pieces vertically. Spread about 3 tablespoons of cream sauce on bottom of plate. Place slice of cake on top of cream sauce. Top slice of cake with caramel sauce. For dramatic presentation, place cream sauce on plate. Put caramel sauce into clean condiment dispenser (squeeze container with hole in the top - usually for mustard and/or catsup.) Pour concentric circles of caramel in cream sauce. With point of toothpick, run "lines" from center of plate to outer edge of plate. Turn plate slightly and repeat every 3/4 inch or so until you make a decorative spider web pattern. Then put slice of cake in middle of plate and garnish with fresh peach slice and mint.

PREP TIME for cake: 20 minutes.
COOK TIME for cake: 55 minutes.
PREP TIME for cream sauce:
3 minutes.
COOK TIME for cream sauce:
30 minutes.
PREP TIME for caramel sauce:
5 minutes.
COOK TIME for caramel sauce:
20 minutes.

TESTED RECIPE

PER SERVING: 311 CALORIES ❦ 16G FAT (46% CALORIES FROM FAT) ❦ 3G PROTEIN
40G CARBOHYDRATE ❦ 92MG CHOLESTEROL ❦ 68MG SODIUM

Idella's House by the Guadalupe River

"Idella was fragile yet beautiful, like old porcelain. She could have been the mother of a lesser pharaoh. Her skin was pale olive, nearly translucent. Her eyes were bright and gray and deep. She was very old now. Yet Idella had always been old. As I entered her house I felt a child in her presence; I felt again that curious blend of awe, respect, and fear; a sense that Idella knew all the secrets of the universe."

Few places on earth could be as magical to a child as where the Guadalupe River bottoms cut deep around Idella's house behind Court Street in Seguin, Texas. It was said Idella's ability to see into the worlds of the future and past was unfailing. She could predict with absolute accuracy the month and day certain people would be married.

I was eight years old and new to town when I first met Idella. It was a few weeks before Christmas, in front of the candy counter at Duke & Ayers, the local five-and-dime. My Grandma B., Virginia Bergfeld, Miss Bettie's daughter, liked to fill her cut glass bowls with colorful rock candies and peppermints for the holidays. Every year Grandma B. took me along for this part of her shopping. As we stood there in front of the dazzling temptations, Grandma B. and Idella exchanged warm greetings. They were lifelong neighbors, Grandma B. explained, as she introduced me to Idella, and she told Idella that I was her neighbor now too, living with my mother and father in the Bettie King home. Idella told me that she had known Miss Bettie all her life and that she was a fine woman.

On the way home, Grandma B. pointed out the white picket fence and Idella's neat little house above the river bottoms where the Guadalupe cuts back almost to Court Street. She also told me Idella had abilities as a fortune teller that were absolutely *uncanny*.

For years after, whenever I crossed the bridges over the King Branch on my way to town, I always sneaked a peek. Sometimes I saw Idella on her porch and she would wave. Other times people had parked their big cars outside Idella's house and I wondered about the woman they were visiting, the mysterious old black woman they said could talk with the dead and whose greatest gift was finding things lost.

Idella Lampkin made a comfortable living from fortune telling. And whatever you may have heard

Idella Lampkin, fortune teller

about other fortune tellers, she was a churchgoing, God-fearing woman. Indeed, she sometimes revealed the awesome visionary foresight of an Old Testament prophet.

My own great-aunt, Nellie DeLaney King, received a prophecy from Idella, but only in hindsight did she recognize its fearsome power.

Nellie DeLaney had married George King, Grandma B.'s brother, and their home was a few blocks up Court Street from Miss Bettie King's. When she was pregnant for the fourth time, Aunt Nellie went to Idella. Now remember, this was many years before a doctor could tell you if a baby would be a girl or a boy. Idella told Aunt Nellie flat out, "You will have two sons."

But Nellie King was unbelieving. "Now Idella," she said sternly, "You are not making sense. You know that I already have a daughter and two sons, and the doctor told me I'm not going to have twins." Idella stood her ground. "Miss Nellie," she said, "I see you with two sons."

Aunt Nellie left Idella's house and told everyone in the family that the famed fortune teller had failed to see her future. Her baby turned out to be a boy, giving her a daughter and three sons. But before the year ended, Nellie's daughter, Mary Ann, was killed in a tragic car accident, and not so many years later the body of her oldest son, George Henry King, was brought home from Okinawa after World War II.

Aunt Nellie lived on into her nineties. For almost half a century and for more than half her life, she enjoyed the love and support of my cousins Donald and Kenneth King, her two surviving sons. The two sons Idella "saw."

Perhaps because Idella's clients were not always pleased to pay for revelations that would not prove true until years had gone by, she learned to supplement her psychic gifts. In her fortune-telling sessions,

So I began my search. I interviewed surviving relatives, studied letters, diaries, maps, census records, death certificates, land grants. I began to piece together an authentic version of stories I'd heard as a child. In almost every detail, oral tradition and the historical record were identical. But the stories were incomplete. So I went back to find Idella.

Mary Ann Fritz, slumber party hostess

Idella could provide insights of an everyday nature that nevertheless amazed those who sought her counsel.

In doing my research for *True Women*, I learned how Idella drew on a news-gathering organization larger than the local newspapers could claim. What I found out about her work, from talking to her grand-daughter Sara Harris, among others, in no way reduced my admiration for her fortune-telling skills.

Of course, I had heard that in the old days most white folks treat-ed the blacks around them as if they were invisible, simply forgetting that their black employees had eyes and ears and brains. The maids, the drivers, and the other workers could get a bit of payback by sharing overheard secrets with Idella, or with her intelligence agents.

Elizabeth Miller was one of Idella's reporters. She has been a friend of our family since the days when her father, Abraham Lincoln Miller, worked as a tenant farmer for my great-grandfather Henry King for 45 years. While I was researching *True Women*, she came to my mother's house three times to share her memories with us, and she spoke of Idella with affection and respect.

When she was a little girl in pigtails, Elizabeth Miller recalled, Idella paid her a penny to go around to certain houses and ask the ser-vants how their white folks were doing. She also stopped at the various beauty parlors, and even sat down on the curb outside the barbershops to catch a scrap of news. Elizabeth Miller would then inform Idella about what she had picked up—if anyone had been to the doctor, what medicines they were taking, when someone had financial problems, or if a trip was planned. Idella even heard the important news about the out-of-town relatives of the Seguin folks.

Another industrious intelligence agent was Mr. Sing Lee, the Chinese laundryman who lived and worked across from Idella on Court Street. In his business he went house to house, often sitting in a kitchen

or on a porch while the womenfolk gathered up their dirty linens. From these customers, families who did not have servants to do their washing, Sing Lee would learn who was bedsick, or if someone who had lost at cards was not making good his IOUs, or when a starched shirt was needed for an important coming event.

The murder of Sing Lee was the town's first unsolved homicide, according to Leroy Schneider, a longtime chief of police in Seguin. The usual possible motives were present: It could have been a hate crime, or a robbery gone bad, or perhaps Sing Lee had come to know too much.

Elizabeth Miller had told me, "all the High Sheriffs from around here consulted with Idella," seeking any leads she could provide when they had a crime on their hands. So when my mother and I went to lunch with the retired police chief at Friedeck's, a popular spot for home-style cooking in Seguin, I planned to question him about the relationship between the area lawmen and the local psychic. First I asked about Peachtree, a hermit who lived in the river bottoms behind Idella's house. Chief Schneider confirmed my guess that the two had been friends. He had often observed them talking out by the back gate in her picket fence. But he said he knew little more than I did about Peachtree. The poor man was harmless, he agreed. From the point of view of the police, the worst problem was that at least once a day the wanderings of the bearded old man with a chained owl on his shoulder would set every dog in town to ferocious barking.

Chief Schneider called Idella Lampkin a God-fearing woman, and an upstanding citizen. Her cooperation had often been invaluable, and as long as Idella was alive, Seguin could boast that only one murder had

Idella closed her eyes and seemed to look inward through the years.

"I see you girls taking those car keys out of Mary Ann Fritz's mother's purse and leavin' the slumber party on a night dark as this. Rollin' that car whisper quiet down the drive and into the street, so Miz Fritz can't hear.

I see you girls in your babydoll pajamas so innocent and new and filled with the power of youth."

Idella looked up from my palm, then into my eyes. "It's a dangerous thing to ask. Not just to talk with the dead, but to bring the dead alive. Once you bring them alive they become part of you."

gone unsolved. And he said Idella's gift for finding things lost was absolutely *uncanny*.

I challenged Chief Schneider about the fortune teller, teasingly playing the role of disbeliever. He responded by telling me about one incident he had seen with his own eyes, "When I was just a deputy, way back when, the men in Seguin got to gambling one night downstairs in the basement of the Silver Dollar."

Chief Schneider continued, "One day after an all-night party, the mayor discovered that his beautiful diamond ring was missing. He was terribly upset, because he had inherited that big diamond from his daddy. So we rushed over to Idella's."

"I was driving the mayor," Chief Schneider recalled. "The fortune teller didn't seem surprised to see us, and when the mayor asked her about his ring she replied, 'Aw, that ring is in the Cadillac Bar in Nuevo Laredo.' With that information we took off, shooting down the road to the Mexico border in that big old police car. Sure enough, the mayor found his ring there, and he got it back!"

As we were leaving the cafe, my mother said to me in her sternest school teacher whisper, "Don't you dare tell that story in your book. The mayor's family will not want to read about any wild parties that ended up in some fancy bar in Mexico!"

I tried to argue back that the Chief hadn't said that the mayor himself had ended up in questionable circumstances, only that his heirloom ring had gone astray, and maybe the ring had been stolen, and anyway, the Cadillac Bar was not a place of ill repute. "Well, just don't," my mother replied, with some finality. So I didn't, though I was sorely tempted.

A few years later, I listened as my mother gave a speech about the research that had gone into *True Women*. I knew her favorite subject in these programs was "all the stories the editor made us leave out" to

keep the book down to fewer than 500 pages. This day she told her audience that some of the stories edited out had illustrated Idella's remarkable
gift. My mother added that since *True Women* was published, everyone
in Seguin has come to her with another Idella story.

Sure enough, afterward a nice-looking woman came up, and
reminded me that we had been friends back in our youth. "What you
wrote about Idella's psychic abilities is
certainly true," my friend said. Then
with great enthusiasm she shared a
version of a story told in her family
about Idella: "Why, my uncle once
lost an heirloom diamond ring, and he
went to Idella for help. He told us that
Idella knew right where it was—in the
bottom of his sock drawer!" Hearing
this particular Idella story really made
me smile, because my friend's uncle,
for more than twenty years, had been
a popular mayor of Seguin.

Idella's visitors usually remem-
bered what they had been told. At a book signing in Plano, a woman
picked up a copy of *True Women*, turned a few pages, and screamed,
"IDELLA! I KNEW HER!" When she recovered her composure, she
hurried to tell me she had grown up in Luling, a few miles from my
hometown. She believed to this day that Idella Lampkin had special
powers, and she told this story to back up her point.

A few weeks before finishing high school, the woman said, she had gone to visit Idella with a couple of friends to have their fortunes told. Idella hesitated. But the girls urged her on, "Oh, please, please—come on." Idella said she could only see something for two of them, and nothing for the third. That girl wanted to leave immediately, but the others sat down to learn what would become of their boyfriends, about the weddings and children to come, and more. Together the friends returned to the little town of Luling, laughing about it all. But a few days after their trip to Seguin, the one girl whose future Idella balked at telling was crossing some railroad tracks and was killed by a train.

I never went to Idella to have my future foretold. Maybe because my parents were college educated—you know, scientific and skeptical; or maybe because I never quite overcame my childhood awe of her. But when I went off to college, and was just a freshman at the University of Texas, I went with my roommate, Mary Kaye Fenwick, to visit Austin's famous fortune teller, Madame Hipple. Of course, I remember only some of what she told me. Perhaps I soon forgot all the things she told me that were proven wrong.

But I was duly impressed when Madame Hipple told me the "W" would be the most important letter of the alphabet for me. I had not told her that my last name was Woods, that my father was named Wilton, and my only brother was named Wilton too. Of course, that was before I had even met Wayne Windle—though I married him just a year or so later—before our oldest son Wayne Wilton Windle was born, or our first two grandsons William Wayne Windle and John Wilton Windle. It was many long years before I signed my name, Janice Woods Windle, on *True Women*.

I also took note when Madame Hipple examined my hand, found a diamond pattern, and told me I would become "famous." Oh, murder!—I'd wanted to hear her say "rich."

I am often asked why I chose Idella Lampkin for the role in *True*

Idella said, "It's just that you found what you came to find. That's all. You're not just pieces anymore, you're a whole cloth. A Texas Star quilt God made with pieces of your grandmothers."

"Where are they now?" I asked Idella. "They're all here, honey. Like I told you, everybody that was, still is. To call them, all you have to do is say their name."

Women. Well, truthfully, I did not exactly choose her.

When I began working with my editor at G. P. Putnam's Sons in New York, he told me I had to find a novelistic device to frame the stories of the main characters. Perhaps I could use the voice of an outsider, he said, somebody who knew them all, someone who could connect their lives and mine. Well, I felt lost. My book was about family, and it already stretched halfway across the state of Texas and all the way to Georgia. How could I find a commentator who knew all these 19th-century women, who knew me, a child of the 20th century—and who was still an outsider? Where would I find somebody with magical powers, someone able to see across time and distance?

That could *only* be Idella, of course.

When I realized I needed Idella Lampkin's help in talking with the dead and finding things lost, it seemed she had been expecting me all along. It was absolutely *uncanny.*

Idella Lampkin's Orange Juice Pie

"THE ONLY SECRETS THERE HAVE EVER BEEN IN
THIS PART OF TEXAS ARE THE ONES GOD KEEPS.
AND I'M MAKIN' A LITTLE PROGRESS ON THOSE."

Servings: 8

1   pie crust (9 inch)
     baked and cooled
14   ounces sweetened condensed
     milk (1 can)
1/2 cup frozen orange juice
     concentrate, thawed
1   cup orange sections, chopped
1   tablespoon Grand Marnier
     or Cointreau
1   cup heavy cream, whipped
     pinch salt

In a large bowl, combine all ingredients except pie crust and whipped cream. Fold in whipped cream. Pour into prepared pie crust and freeze until firm, at least six hours. Keep any remaining pie stored in freezer, covered. Garnish with fresh mint leaves just before serving. ❧

PREP TIME: 30 minutes.

TESTED RECIPE
PER SERVING: 398 CALORIES ❧ 21G FAT (48% CALORIES FROM FAT) ❧ 6G PROTEIN
46G CARBOHYDRATE ❧ 58 MG CHOLESTEROL ❧ 220 MG SODIUM

Granny Rachel Boyd's Advice
"WITH HER SETTIN' HEN WEDDING GIFT"

HOW TO REMOVE LICE AND MITES FROM CHICKENS:

Pour two ounces of sheep dip into an extra large pail of water. Give each fowl a good sousing dip, feet first, up to the neck, and then inverting, a mercifully swift head plunge, after which it is tossed, gasping, sneezing and half-blinded, out onto the soft clean grass.

Be careful to attend to this chore on a mild sunny day when the feathers can dry. You will notice that after only a few minutes of gagging and staggering the birds find their feet all right and begin to eat and scratch as if nothing ever happened.

*Janice Woods
Seguin High, 1956
Seguin, Tx*

Slumber Party Cherry Cookies

"SERVED TO THE TRUE WOMEN
IN THE CLASS OF '56"

Servings: 48

1 3/4	cups flour, sift before measuring
1	egg
1/2	teaspoon salt
1	cup shortening
2/3	cup sugar
1	teaspoon vanilla
1/2	cup maraschino cherries, drained and chopped

Preheat oven to 400 degrees. Sift flour, measure, add salt, and sift again. Cream shortening and add sugar gradually, blending until light. Add egg and beat well. Stir flour mixture into batter. Then add vanilla and cherries. Mix well. Chill well, about one hour. Form balls about 1 1/2 inches in diameter and place on ungreased cookie sheet. Bake for 10 minutes or until cookies brown lightly. Keep dough in refrigerator when not in use (between batches). 🌿

PREP TIME: 35 minutes.
CHILL TIME: 1 hour.
ROLLING TIME FOR EACH BATCH: 10 minutes.

*Wayne Windle
Texas High, 1955
Texarkana, Tx*

TESTED RECIPE

PER SERVING: 68 CALORIES ❦ 4G FAT (56% CALORIES FROM FAT) ❦ 0G PROTEIN
7G CARBOHYDRATE ❦ 0MG CHOLESTEROL ❦ 24MG SODIUM

Oranges with Caramel Sauce

"FOR MAYOR ZORN'S BIRTHDAY"

Servings: 6

6	oranges, large
1 1/2	cups brown sugar, packed
1/2	cup plus
2	tablespoons whipping cream
1/2	teaspoon salt
3/4	cup butter

For Garnish:

1/2	cup whipping cream
1/2	cup chopped pecans

PREP TIME FOR ORANGES:

18 minutes.

TIME TO WHIP CREAM:

5 to 8 minutes.

ASSEMBLY TIME:

15 minutes.

For sauce, combine brown sugar, 1/2 cup plus 2 tablespoons whipping cream, salt and butter in saucepan. Cook on medium-high heat and bring to a boil, stirring constantly. Boil for 2 minutes. Remove from heat and allow to cool. Refrigerate until chilled and sauce thickens. Meanwhile, prepare oranges. Peel oranges, making sure to remove as much pith (white part) as possible, as this is where the bitterness in citrus fruit is concentrated. Slice oranges horizontally, each slice about 1/2 inch thick. For individual presentation, layer orange slices in a pretty wine glass, parfait glass, or goblet. Over each layer of orange slices, spoon 2 tablespoons of sauce. Top sauce with about one tablespoon of chopped pecans. Continue to layer orange slices, sauce, and nuts. Each glass should have the equivalent of one whole orange in slices and 3 teaspoons of both caramel and pecans. Beat remaining 1/2 cup whipping cream until stiff, and dollop on top of orange slices. Sprinkle whipped cream with remaining nuts and serve immediately. Can be presented in a large trifle bowl or other glass container. Serve using a large spoon.

Delicious served with a glass of Cointreau or Grand Marnier. For a twist on this recipe, steep the orange slices in Grand Marnier for about thirty minutes before layering! All components of this dish can be prepared ahead of time, but assembly should be just before service.

TESTED RECIPE

PER SERVING: 221 CALORIES ❦ 11G FAT (37% CALORIES FROM FAT) ❦ 2G PROTEIN
39G CARBOHYDRATE ❦ 27MG CHOLESTEROL ❦ 18MG SODIUM

Aunt Nona's Eggnog

"SHE TOLD ME ALL THE WOODS FAMILY SAGAS"

Beat 12 eggs until light in color. Gradually beat in 2 cups confectioners sugar (or more to taste), 1/2 teaspoon salt, and 1 teaspoon vanilla. Stir in 1 1/2 quarts whole milk, 1 quart heavy whipping cream (unwhipped), 6 cups bourbon, 2 cups rum or brandy. Refrigerate several hours before serving, the longer the better.

Servings: 4

12	eggs
2	cups confectioners sugar (or more to taste)
1/2	teaspoon salt
1	teaspoon vanilla
1 1/2	quarts whole milk
1	quart heavy whipping cream (unwhipped)
6	cups bourbon
2	cups rum or brandy

Moss Ranch Dessert

"FOR THE DOUBLE WEDDING OF BETTIE AND NUGE"

In a large glass bowl, layer first five ingredients in the order given above, beginning with walnuts and ending with pecans. Whip cream only until it reaches the consistency of a sauce. Pour whipping cream over layered ingredients. Cover and allow to chill overnight. To serve, spoon into individual serving bowls. Makes 12 servings of 3/4 cups each.

Servings: 12

2	cups walnuts, chopped
2	cups dates, chopped
2	cups maraschino cherries, chopped
18	mashmallows, cut into pieces, about 2 cups
2	cups pecans, chopped
2	cups whipping cream

TESTED RECIPE

PER SERVING: 580 CALORIES ❦ 24G FAT (36% CALORIES FROM FAT) ❦ 5G PROTEIN
94G CARBOHYDRATE ❦ 54MG CHOLESTEROL ❦ 69MG SODIUM

"Granny Boyd was constantly campaigning for a new church building. 'How can the town grow without a church!' she would say, and then, with a wink, blame most everything on the Texas Rangers. 'I swear this town has more Texas Rangers than you can shake a stick at. Just about the time we start to make some progress, off they go chasing Indians or outlaws, real or imagined.'"

The little house where Granny Boyd spent her last days alone was officially pronounced substandard. The city officials said it had to go.

To me, that tiny home on East Mountain Street had always been there. It was there when I went to Mary B. Erskine Elementary School, and there when I pedaled past it on my way to visit my friend Mary Telva Fischer. Even a fresh coat of bright yellow paint that matched the voluptuous yellow blossoms of the nearby fearsome prickly pear cactus couldn't hide its age. The home had always been there and always would be.

Aren't houses like that to be cherished forever? Aren't they for people to live in and pass along to the next generation...and the next?

In 1840, Rachel King, a widow with three sons in Tennessee, married J.A.M. Boyd, a much younger man whose wife had died, leaving him with several children. Rachel's two oldest sons, Henry and John King, had left years before for Texas, settling on the banks of the Guadalupe River in the community that became Seguin.

By 1842, Rachel, her youngest son William King, and her new family followed Henry and John to Texas. They, too, settled in Seguin on the banks of the Guadalupe. The frontier community had barely a dozen houses when they arrived, but it didn't take long for them to make it their home.

Granny Rachel Boyd left her mark on this town. She registered her own cattle brand at the courthouse on September 26, 1842. And it was here that she began a legendary practice, giving a setting hen to

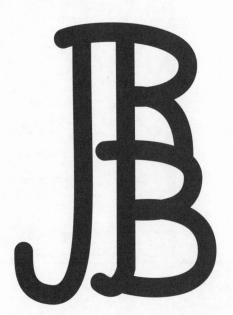

Granny Boyd registered her cattle brand on September 26, 1846.

every bride—along with advice on how a woman could earn a little money on her own, and thus keep a bit of independence.

Granny Boyd was the first to teach Sunday school in Seguin, gathering the children under the great oaks in the heart of this raw-boned settlement during the nearly year-long warm months. By 1849, she and her fellow townspeople built their first church where they could meet for prayer and worship. In 1850, Rachel Boyd watched her youngest son, William George King, marry Euphemia Texas Ashby in that first church.

In frontier ecumenicalism, the local Methodists who built the simple church shared it with their neighbors and with visiting preachers— Baptists, Presbyterians, or Episcopalians, as well as Methodist circuit riders. The townspeople called it the First Church. It had one door for gentlemen, another for ladies.

No matter who was preaching, Granny Boyd never missed a service, always sitting in the very first pew on the side reserved for women only. Next to the pulpit, Uncle Billy Pitts sat in the Amen Corner, leading the congregation in emphatic agreement with the preacher's fervent sermonizing by exclaiming, "Amen!"

But during the long hours of preaching, Uncle Billy, from his spot beside the preacher and facing the congregation,

First Church of Seguin.

In 1850, Rachel Boyd watched her youngest son, William George King, marry Euphemia Texas Ashby in that first church.

sometimes let his gaze linger on the comely ladies facing him. Indeed, some said Granny Boyd took up her position in the front pew to keep an eye on Uncle Billy. She knew the strong temptations of the flesh could weaken a churchgoing man.

With that thought in mind, she warned her daughter-in-law, Euphemia, "Even preachers have roving hands."

In 1990, what appeared to be a run-down old duplex on a run-down street in Seguin was under threat of government regulations. (Why do new regulations always seem so hostile to old buildings?)

There was something very special about this old structure, but its past, like Granny Boyd's little yellow house, was invisible to the untrained eye. In a reckless "modernization" effort, the double front doors, one door for gentlemen and one for ladies, had been made into separate doors leading to duplex apartments. Its modest steeple had been removed. Then along came new zoning regulations concerning density and appropriate use, and the old structure appeared to be in serious violation. It was in danger of destruction.

At that moment, local historians recognized the rare provenance of the old building. The Seguin Conservation Society began raising the funds in 1993, first to buy it, then to move it, and finally to restore it.

Today, First Church has been rescued and restored. It is a treasure some century and a half in years and is once again in a place of honor.

Amen! As Uncle Billy would have said.

On the other side of town, a little home that had a streak of faded yellow paint still stood. It had given shelter to people of modest means and needs until 1992. The gently sagging covered porch had protected them from the burning sun and the chilling rain, while the walls were a shield against the cutting wind.

But the house was worn with age...and vacant.

One man was trying to make it a house fit to rent again. With his own carpentry, he had firmed up the roof, refreshed the walls with paint, and had plans to install new plumbing and wiring. Unfortunately, he needed more money than he had to pay for the materials. He appealed to the officials to give him more time.

He got no more time. He understood the orders; the structure had been declared substandard. Without all-new plumbing and all-new wiring, it would have to go. And if he could not finish the repairs by the deadline, or if he did not demolish the house himself, the city would do it for him and send him the bill.

Granny Boyd's precious jewel of a house was more than 100 years old when it was condemned and destroyed. In its place is an empty lot. That charming stretch of East Mountain Street now reminds me of a ring that has lost its center stone.

From the rubble of demolition, my mother rescued the screen-door frames, full of gingerbread ornamentation so popular long ago. She had those pieces made into a new screendoor for her back porch and, in telling the stories of *True Women*, we were able to preserve some fragments of history from Granny Boyd's life.

What can we do to save more of the humble homes, the kind where our ancestors lived out their lives?

Once, my beautiful hometown of Seguin had so many old homes we simply took them for granted, only to wake up and find many were gone. Perhaps we thought that because they had survived for so many decades, much like their aged owners, they would always be there.

No, Sam Houston did not dine here. George Washington never slept here. Only good-hearted American families lived on East Mountain Street. No family can ever live in it again.

Granny Boyd's house is gone.

No, Sam Houston did not dine here. George Washington never slept here. Only good-hearted American families lived on East Mountain Street. No family can ever live in it again.

Granny Boyd's house is gone.

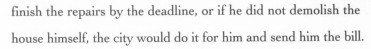

Little Virginia's Texas Sunshine Salad Dressing

"SO GOOD YOU'LL WANT TO EAT IT WITH A SPOON"

Servings:
10 - 1/4 cup servings of salad dressing
5 - 1/2 cup servings of frozen dessert

	juice of one freshly squeezed orange
	juice of one freshly squeezed lemon
1/4	*cup pineapple juice*
2	*egg yolks*
3/4	*cup sugar*
1	*tablespoon flour*
1/2	*teaspoon salt*
1/2	*teaspoon prepared mustard*
1	*dozen marshmallows, cut into pieces*
1	*cup whipping cream, whipped*

Heat juices in top of double boiler. In a separate bowl, beat yolks. Temper yolks by adding a little of the hot juices to yolks, beating constantly. Slowly add tempered yolks back into juices in top of double boiler, whisking constantly. Add flour and whisk. Add sugar, mustard and salt. Cook until thickened, stirring constantly. Remove from heat and strain mixture into another bowl. Add marshmallows to strained sauce and stir until marshmallows melt. Allow mixture to cool thoroughly before folding in whipped cream. Chill. ❦

Can be used as a dressing for a salad of avocado and grapefruit slices or can be frozen in champagne flutes and served as a frozen dessert, almost like an ice cream. Garnish with fresh mint.

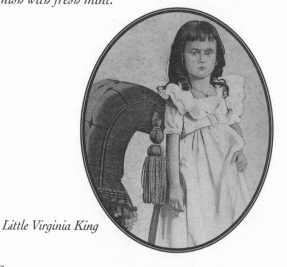

Little Virginia King

TESTED RECIPE

PER SERVING: 193 CALORIES ❦ 10G FAT (45% CALORIES FROM FAT) ❦ 2G PROTEIN
26G CARBOHYDRATE ❦ 75MG CHOLESTEROL ❦ 123MG SODIUM

Josephine Battaglia Kemendo's Spaghetti Sauce

"TEXAS ITALIAN SETTLER'S ORIGINAL RECIPE FROM THE 1800's"

Spray large saucepan with nonstick cooking spray. Heat pan and add pork and beef. Salt and pepper meat and sauté until cooked through. Remove meat and drain fat. Spray same saucepan again with nonstick cooking spray and add onions. Salt and pepper onions and sauté until translucent. As onions cook, scrape up any browned bits in bottom of saucepan. When onions are ready, slowly add a little liquid from the crushed tomatoes, and scrape up any remaining browned bits. Add the rest of the tomatoes and the rest of the ingredients. Heat thoroughly, taste and adjust seasonings. Simmer uncovered for 2 hours, stirring occasionally. Remove bay leaf. Taste and adjust seasonings for a final time. Makes 16 servings of 3/4 cup each or 12 cups.

Servings: 16

1/2	pound ground pork
1 1/2	pounds ground beef
1	large onion, chopped
28	ounces canned crushed tomatoes (1 can)
24	ounces tomato paste (4 cans)
4 3/4	teaspoons salt
1	teaspoon pepper
4	teaspoons oregano
1	bay leaf broken in half
1	teaspoon basil
	pinch sugar
	dash cinnamon, or to taste
4 1/2	cups water

PREP TIME: 40 minutes.
COOK TIME: 2 hours.

Sauce is best when made the day before serving. Freezes well.

TESTED RECIPE

PER SERVING: 150 CALORIES 9G FAT (53% CALORIES FROM FAT) 9G PROTEIN
9G CARBOHYDRATE 31MG CHOLESTEROL 742MG SODIUM

Every Sunday After Church Chicken

"FOR MY WILLIAM AND JOHN"

Servings: 4

1	3 1/2 pound chicken, quartered
1	tablespoon extra virgin olive oil
1	bunch green onions, thinly sliced. Separate white from green tops.
4	ounces mushrooms, sliced
1	large shallot, chopped fine
1	bay leaf
8	ounces cream cheese, room temperature
1	can cream of mushroom soup
2/3	cup white wine
	salt and pepper to taste
	cayenne and paprika to taste
1/4	teaspoon garlic powder

Preheat oven to 350. Clean and quarter chicken, and liberally season with salt, pepper, cayenne and paprika. In a large, deep skillet, heat olive oil over medium-high heat. Quickly brown chicken on both sides. Remove chicken from skillet and set aside in 9" x 13" pan. Reduce heat to medium and sauté white parts of green onion and mushrooms with salt, pepper and garlic powder. Cook until mushrooms release liquids and then add finely chopped shallots. Cook for about 3 to 5 minutes. Do not overcook or mushrooms will lose their texture. Add cream cheese, soup and wine. Break bay leaf in half and add. Stir until blended and cream cheese melts. Taste and adjust seasonings (it probably needs about 1/4 teaspoon salt, 1/4 teaspoon pepper, and cayenne). Stir and add green onion tops. Pour over browned chicken and bake uncovered, for 1 hour, or until juices from chicken run clear. Remove bay leaf before serving. Gravy is delicious over Texas basmati rice. Complete your dinner with fresh steamed asparagus and a tomato and yellow bell pepper salad. Serve with a dry white wine like a Viognier. ❧

PREP TIME: 40 minutes.
COOK TIME: 1 hour 30 minutes.

TESTED RECIPE

PER SERVING: 743 CALORIES ❧ 44G FAT (55% CALORIES FROM FAT) ❧ 67G PROTEIN
13G CARBOHYDRATE ❧ 248MG CHOLESTEROL ❧ 614MG SODIUM

East Mountain Street Cake

"SOME OF THE BEST COOKS AND PRETTIEST HOUSES ARE ON MOUNTAIN STREET IN SEGUIN"

Miss Helen Bartels

Preheat even to 375 degrees. Grease three 9" round cake pans and line with parchment paper. Melt chocolate in the top of a double boiler. Remove from heat and allow to cool. In a mixing bowl, combine eggs, sugar, and vanilla and mix well, at least 3 minutes. Batter will turn pale yellow. Pour chocolate into mixture. Put soda into buttermilk and mix well. Add buttermilk/soda mixture to batter. Make sure all of the soda has been added to the batter. Do not overbeat. Sift flour into batter and mix until ingredients are just combined. Pour 1/3 of batter into each prepared pan and bake for 15 minutes, or until a toothpick inserted into middle of layer comes out with moist crumbs. DO NOT OVERBAKE.

FOR ICING: Combine chocolate, brown sugar, milk, egg yolk, and vanilla in the top of a double boiler. Cook and stir until icing thickens slightly, about 15 minutes.

TO ASSEMBLE: Allow cakes to cool just enough to remove from pan without breaking. Peel off parchment paper. Place one layer top side down on serving platter. Pour 1/3 of icing on layer. Repeat with next layer. Then place third layer top down on other two layers. Spread pecans over top of cake and pour rest of icing over pecans. Allow to cool completely before cutting.

Servings: 12

Cake:

4	ounces unsweetened baking chocolate
5	eggs
2 1/2	cups sugar
2	teaspoons vanilla
1	teaspoon baking soda
1	cup buttermilk
2	cups flour, sifted

Icing:

4	ounces unsweetened baking chocolate
1	cup brown sugar
1	cup milk
1	egg yolk
2	teaspoons vanilla
2/3	cup crushed pecans

CAKE PREP TIME: 30 minutes.

COOK TIME: 40 minutes.

ICING PREP TIME: 10 minutes.

COOK TIME: 15 minutes.

TIME TO ICE CAKE: less than 5 minutes.

TESTED RECIPE

PER SERVING: 456 CALORIES ❧ 16G FAT (29% CALORIES FROM FAT) ❧ 8G PROTEIN
78G CARBOHYDRATE ❧ 96MG CHOLESTEROL ❧ 167MG SODIUM

The Wedding Gift

Janice King Woods Becomes Brid Of Wayne Windle Jr. in Segui

Miss Janice King Woods, daughter of Mr. and Mrs. Wilton Woods of Seguin, Texas became the bride of Wayne Windle, Jr., son of Mrs. Wayne Windle Sr., and the late Mr. Windle of Texarkana, Texas. The double ring candle light ceremony was performed at 4 p.m. Sunday, January 26th in the Knolle Chapel of the First Methodist Church in Seguin, Texas. Present were members of the immediate families and close friends.

The Rev. Kermit Gibbons, pastor of the church read the marriage vows and the music was furnished by Mrs. William A. Bergfeld, Jr., aunt of the bride. Numbers selected were "Whither Thou Goest", "Always", and Grieg's Prelude, "I Love Thee," followed by the traditional processional and recessional wedding music.

The chapel was decorated with baskets of white stock set among

man of Ft. Worth as groomsman.

The bride's mother wore a dress of peacock blue peau de soie with hat of matching color of chiffon and milan straw. She pinned a corsage of pink ranunculas to her shoulder. The mother of the bridegroom wore a champagne colored lace dress with petalled hat of champagn velvet and satin flowers. She wore a corsage of rose camellias.

At the closing moments of the exchange of vows the chime bells of the church were rung.

A reception was held at the home of the bride's parents. The table was covered with a handmade lace cloth, made by the mother of the bride. In the center was an arrangement of white stock, ranunculas and candytuft in a silver candle epergne. A four-tiered wedding cake topped with sugar spun with bride's bouquet and ribbon streamers was served by Miss

San Antonio Exp member of Alpha a member of Spo organization for University. The graduate of Texar School. He is a la University where of Sigma Alpha F member of the int cil and member an honorary serv

Out of town gu ding other than tioned were Mr. a A. Bergfeld, Jr. roe, Texas; Mr. Edsel Bergfeld a pus Christi; Mrs. San Marcos; Mr. D. Taylor of Aus of Austin; George ton; Mr. and Mr and Miss Julie P Mr. and Mrs. C.

Wayne and Janice Windle (1958)

The wedding gift scrapbook, filled with family photographs and recipes, was given to our son, Wayne, and his bride, Mary Jane Emmett, on June 6, 1985 at their rehearsal dinner held at our home.

As I watched the bridesmaids and grooms-men hover over the scrapbook asking for the family stories to be read aloud, I realized it was the true stories about the adventures of actual people that they wanted to hear.

In a recent interview, I was asked what I felt was most rewarding about this per-sonal journey since I began to work on a family cookbook.

Of course, it was exhilarating to see the story become a book and then a CBS minis-eries. And a real highpoint was the Library of Congress recommendation of the book for young readers. But, unquestionably, the most fun was working all those years with my mother and many relatives.

"And the future?" the reporter asked.

The real icing on the cake for me would be to see *True Women* encourage more people to write their own family stories.

Emmett - Windle

Mary Jane Emmett a[...]
Wayne Wilton Windle w[...]
married June 7 in Pro-Cat[...]
dral Church of St. Clem[...]
with the Rev. Ron Thoms[...]
officiating.

Her parents are Gabr[...]
Thomas and Jane Emm[...]
His parents are Wayne E. a[...]
Janice Windle.

Marsha E. Daw was matr[...]
of honor and Keith Emm[...]
was maid of honor. Peggy [...]
Powers, Betsy K. Levens[...]
Virginia Windle and S[...]
Sally Harris were brid[...]
maids.

Wayne E. Windle was b[...]
man. Wilton Woods, Char[...]
Windle, Brent Harris, Ha[...]
Hussmann, Grant Bass[...]
Nick Emmett, John Emmett
and Tom Emmett were
groomsmen.

The bride works for Condel[...]
Architects an[...]
is a gradua[...]
High School, [...]
in Arlington, [...]

The bridegroom works fo[...]
Pan American Industria[...]
Group. He is a graduate o[...]

Papa Leonard Moss and Wedding Party

WEDDING

Windle and Shapiro are married

By Don Woodyard

In the summer of 1984, Virginia Laura Windle, through a friend, arranged for an "accidental" meeting with Randy David Shapiro at Gasoline Alley.

"I knew he was going to be there," she recalls. "He thought it was an accidental meeting." Having boned up on the Dallas Cowboys with her father, she discussed the team's quarterback woes with Randy, the man destined to be her husband.

She says she played hard to get and they didn't start dating until two years later. "I thought he was real cute," she adds. They dated for more than four years before they got married

The author and her parents

Bettie King

Woody Woods

Charlie Windle

The Wedding Gift section is a replica of the photographs and recipes submitted by relatives and friends for the original scrapbook. The recipes are reprinted here as they were given to me, and the main thing I can vouch for is—they are delicious.

Grandma B.'s Apple Salad

"VIRGINIA IS NAMED FOR HER. SHE WAS A WONDERFUL COOK"

Servings: 6

1	egg
1	cup milk
	sugar to taste
	pinch of salt
3	large apples, chopped
2	cups celery, chopped
2	cups pecan halves

Beat egg, milk, sugar (about 1/4 cup) and pinch of salt. Allow these ingredients to come to a boil in the top of a double boiler. Avoid stirring. Cool. Pour mixture over apples, celery and pecan halves. Chill well. ❧

Marjorie Parker's Escalloped Asparagus

"MOTHER OF THAT NAUGHTY PARKER GIRL"

Peggy Parker

Servings: 12

2	cups canned asparagus, chopped
6	hard-boiled eggs
1/4	cheese (any type that melts well)
1	tablespoon flour
1	tablespoon butter
2	cups crushed potato chips

Drain juice from asparagus and save. Place asparagus in baking dish. Make a sauce by melting the butter and cheese together, adding the juice of the asparagus. Stir in the flour. Cook sauce until thickened. Pour over the asparagus. Garnish with slices of hard-boiled eggs. (If you prefer, use only the egg whites). Top with crushed potato chips. Bake in a moderate oven until brown. ❧

Cecil Windle's Coca-Cola Salad

"FOR HIGH SCHOOL HOMECOMING POT LUCK SUPPER"

Drain juices from cherries and pineapple and add to fruit juice. Boil together for 3 minutes and remove from heat. Pour in gelatin and stir well. When mixture is cool, pour in the 2 Coca-Colas. Chill in refrigerator for 30 minutes. Fold the fruit, cherries, pineapples and nuts into partially congealed mixture. Stir well. Pour into a clear glass bowl so that the wine red color and floating fruit may be seen in the salad.

1	14 ounce can Bing cherries
1	large can crushed pineapple
2	cups apple or raspberry juice
1	package cherry gelatin
2	bottles of Classic Coca-Cola
1	cup nuts, chopped

Cecil Windle

Bride's First Party Casserole

Servings: 6

4	large chicken breasts, skinned and boned
2	pounds cooked, peeled medium shrimp
1/2	cup water
	salt and pepper
2	10 ounce packages, frozen leaf spinach
1	8 ounce package cream cheese, cubed
1/2	cup white wine
1	10 ounce can cream of mushroom soup
1	10 ounce can cream of celery soup
2	tablespoons butter
2	tablespoons grated Parmesan cheese
1/4	teaspoon pepper
1/4	teaspoon garlic powder
2	tablespoons dry bread crumbs

For Garnish:

1	lemon, thinly sliced
1/2	cup fresh parsley, coarsely chopped

Season chicken with salt and pepper. Bake or cook the chicken breasts in a crockpot with about 1/2 cup of water until they are very tender and can be pulled apart or cut into bite-size pieces. Chop the cooked shrimp and combine with pieces of chicken breast.

Separately: Cook spinach and drain off juice. Combine cream cheese and butter and cook in a saucepan until melted. Remove from the heat and add the spinach to the cream cheese mixture. Stir. Add wine, soups, Parmesan cheese, pepper and garlic powder, and stir well. Lightly grease 12" x 8" x 2" baking dish. Spoon in spinach mixture and fold in shrimp and chicken, stirring to combine spinach, shrimp and chicken breasts. Sprinkle bread crumbs over the top. Bake 350 degrees for 30 to 40 minutes. Garnish with parsley and lemon slices just before serving.

Charlie's Birthday Treat

CRABMEAT ALMONDINE—"YOUR LITTLE BROTHER'S FAVORITE DISH"

Go through crabmeat to pick out the shells. Try to keep the lumps of crabmeat intact. Lightly salt and pepper green and red bell peppers and sauté in melted butter about 4-5 minutes. Remove from heat and stir in arrowroot. Combine milk and 1/3 cup water. Add to the butter and arrowroot mixture. Return to heat, stirring slowly until thick and smooth, about 10 minutes. Stir in chervil, celery, almonds and crabmeat. (If you do not like the idea of almonds in the crabmeat, the almonds can be placed on top of the cheese with the breadcrumbs just before baking.) Taste and adjust seasonings, adding about 3/4 teaspoon salt and 1/8 teaspoon cayenne. Pour into a 1 1/2 quart casserole or into individual shell ramekins. Top with shredded cheese and then with buttered bread crumbs. Bake at 350 for 30-35 minutes until the cheese is melted. ❧

PREP TIME: 45 minutes
COOK TIME: 30 minutes

Two things are critical to this dish: picking out any small bits of shell in the crabmeat and proper seasoning.

Servings: 6

1	pound crabmeat; lump, if possible
1	tablespoon chopped green bell pepper
1/4	cup butter
4	teaspoons arrowroot
1	cup evaporated milk
1/3	cup water
	salt and pepper to taste
1/2	teaspoon chervil or to taste
1/2	cup celery, thinly sliced
2	tablespoons red bell pepper, chopped
1/8	teaspoon cayenne pepper, or to taste
1/2	cup toasted almonds, slivered
1/2	cup bread crumbs buttered
1/2	cup grated cheddar cheese

TESTED RECIPE

PER SERVING: 353 CALORIES ❧ 21G FAT (54% CALORIES FROM FAT) ❧ 24G PROTEIN
16G CARBOHYDRATES ❧ 110MG CHOLESTEROL ❧ 512MG SODIUM

Aunt Maxine's Honey Bunch Beans

"SHE CALLS EVERYONE HONEY BUNCH"

Servings: 6

2	16 ounce cans pork and beans
1/2	white onion, finely chopped
2	tablespoons butter or margarine, melted
1/2	cup molasses
1/2	cup honey
1/4	cup bourbon
1/4	cup strong black coffee, brewed
2	tablespoons bottled red chili sauce
1/4	cup brown sugar
4	strips fried bacon, crumbled
1	16 ounce can pineapple chunks or crushed pineapple

Combine all of the ingredients together with the baked beans. Bake 1 1/2 hours in oven at 375 degrees.

Maxine and Virgil Halm

Aunt Tot's Angel Food Heavenly Fluff

"ANTONIA PAULINE LOUISE BERGFELD, BORN FEBRUARY 1886 IN GUADALUPE COUNTY"

Bake one Angel Food Cake.

STEP ONE: For lemon sauce put ingredients in double boiler top, cook slowly and stir occasionally. When mixture is thick, remove from heat and cool.

STEP TWO: Mix in small bowl. Add to lemon sauce and let cool.

STEP THREE: Mix ingredients and add to lemon mixture. Break apart cake into cube pieces and combine with sauce, alternating layers of cake and lemon sauce in pretty bowl. Chill in icebox at least 3 hours before serving. ❧

Servings: 20

For Sauce:

Step One:

6	eggs
3/4	cup sugar
3/4	cup lemon juice
	rind of 2 lemons, grated
1/4	teaspoon salt

Step Two:

1	envelope gelatin, dissolved
1	cup hot water

Step Three:

6	egg whites, beaten stiff, add
3/4	cup sugar and stir
2	cups whipping cream,

add:

2	tablespoons powdered sugar
1	teaspoon vanilla

William Bergfeld

Laura Hoge Woods' Hill Country Crabapple Jelly

"SHE WAS BORN AT THE HEADWATERS OF THE BLANCO RIVER"

Wash 8 pounds firm red crabapples and scrub skins well. Cut crabapples into quarters and remove stem ends. Cover with cold water and cook rapidly until apples are soft. Strain through several thicknesses of cheese cloth, press the bag gently to start flow of juice.

Never make up more than 4 to 6 cups of juice at a time. To each cup of juice add one cup of sugar. Boil rapidly until the juice sheets from the spoon.

Let stand a minute or two, remove the scum, and pour it into hot sterilized glasses. Add 4 to 5 cloves and a stick of cinnamon.

When set, cover with melted paraffin, label and store in cool, dry place. 🌾

A very antique recipe.

Laura's little boys, Clifford and Wilton

Helen and Joe Fleming's Pear Bread

"A CAPOTE ROAD CLASSIC"

Preheat oven to 325 degrees. Grease a 9" x 5" x 3" loaf pan. Cream margarine and sugar. Add eggs and sour cream and mix. Sift together flour, baking powder, baking soda, and salt. Add to the batter and stir to mix. Add lemon rind, chopped pears, almond extract, milk and nuts and mix well. Pour into prepared pan and bake for 1 hour and 10 minutes or until a toothpick inserted into the center of the loaf comes out almost clean with moist crumbs. Do not overcook. Remove from oven and cool in pan for 10 to 15 minutes. Gently remove from pan. If loaf does not seem to come out easily, allow to cool for 5 or 10 more minutes and try to remove again. Cool completely before serving.

Just before serving, lightly sift powdered sugar over loaf. For special presentation, cut a doily in the shape of the top of the loaf. Place the doily on top of the loaf and then sift the powdered sugar on top. Carefully remove the doily to leave the lacy impression. ❦

PREP TIME: 25 minutes.
COOK TIME: 1 hour 13 minutes.

Delicious with jasmine tea or tea brewed with lots of fresh mint leaves. Remember, only the yellow part of the lemon is the rind. The white part or pith is bitter, so be careful when grating!

Servings: 14

1/2	cup margarine
1 1/3	cups sugar
2	eggs
1/4	cup sour cream
2	cups flour
1 1/2	teaspoons baking powder
1/2	teaspoon baking soda
1/4	teaspoon salt
1	teaspoon grated lemon rind
1	cup chopped pears
1	teaspoon almond extract
2	tablespoons milk
1 1/2	cups chopped pecans

TESTED RECIPE

PER SERVING: 264 CALORIES ❦ 12G FAT (41% CALORIES FROM FAT) ❦ 3G PROTEIN
36G CARBOHYDRATE ❦ 28MG CHOLESTEROL ❦ 209MG SODIUM

Mrs. Lawrence's Apricot Cake

"OUR NEXT DOOR NEIGHBOR WHO BECAME FAMOUS FOR FOUNDING BRICE'S CAFETERIA IN TEXARKANA, TEXAS DURING THE DEPRESSION"

Servings: 15

Cake:

1/2	cup shortening
1	cup sugar
1 1/2	cups cake flour
2	eggs, large
2/3	cup apricots, chopped and stewed
1/2	teaspoon baking soda
1/2	teaspoon salt
1/2	teaspoon nutmeg
1/2	teaspoon baking powder
1/2	teaspoon cinnamon
1/2	teaspoon allspice
2/3	cup buttermilk

Icing:

2	cups powdered sugar
1/2	teaspoon salt
2	tablespoons butter
4	tablespoons apricot jam
1	teaspoon lemon juice
1/2	cup pecans, finely chopped

FOR CAKE: Preheat oven to 350 degrees. Grease 9" x 13" pan. Cream shortening and sugar together. Add flour and mix well. Add eggs, apricots, salt, spices and baking powder, and mix. Add baking soda to buttermilk and stir until soda is dissolved. Pour soda/buttermilk mixture into batter and mix until ingredients are just incorporated. Pour into prepared pan and bake for about 25 minutes or until toothpick inserted into cake comes out with a few moist crumbs. Cooked cake is very delicate. Ice while still hot.

FOR ICING: Mix all ingredients except powdered sugar and pecans. Add sugar and pecans, and beat until creamy.

TO ICE CAKE: Drop icing by 1/2 teaspoonfuls on cake and spread very carefully so as not to tear cake.

PREP TIME for cake: 30 minutes.
BAKE TIME for cake: 25 minutes.
PREP TIME for icing: 10 minutes.

TESTED RECIPE

Mawmaw's Christmas Cake

"THIS ANTIQUE RECIPE IS FROM WAYNE'S FRATERNAL GRANDMOTHER, LILY IRBY WINDLE"

Cream butter with sugar. Beat egg yolks well and stir into the mixture. Add baking soda to buttermilk. Add buttermilk - baking soda mixture to butter, sugar, and egg yolk mixture. Add flour, beating slowly with a free-standing mixer. Add spices and fruits.

Beat egg whites until stiff and fold into above mixture. Add pecans and walnuts. Cook in a deep tube pan at 250 degrees, very slowly for about 10 hours. Allow to cool in pan for about 2 hours. Invert pan onto serving platter and ice with a coating of plum jam to seal in the moisture. 🌿

PREP TIME: 1 hour 30 minutes. COOK TIME: 10 hours. COOL TIME: 2 hours in pan, then several hours after unmolding. TIME TO ICE: 10 minutes. 🌿

Servings: 24

2	sticks butter
1 1/2	cups sugar
3	egg yolks, beaten
1/2	cup buttermilk
1	teaspoon baking soda
3	cups flour
1	tablespoon ground cloves
1	tablespoon cinnamon
1	tablespoon nutmeg
1	tablespoon allspice
1 1/2	cups seedless plum jam
1	pint watermelon jam
1/2	cup pickled watermelon rind, finely chopped
36	maraschino cherries, halved and pitted
1	pint pear preserves
6	ounces raisins, seedless
1	pint apricot preserves (or figs)
8 1/4	ounces crushed pineapple in light syrup, drained
36	chopped dates
1	cup chopped pecans
1	cup walnuts
3	egg whites

Mawmaw's little boys, Wayne and Jewell

TESTED RECIPE

PER SERVING: 1416 CALORIES 🌿 6G FAT (4% CALORIES FROM FAT) 🌿 10G PROTEIN
358G CARBOHYDRATE 🌿 29MG CHOLESTEROL 🌿 278MG SODIUM

Netta Mae Roth's White Star Delight

"IN 1939, FENNER AND NETTA MAE WERE OUR
NEIGHBORS IN SAN ANTONIO."

---

1 1/2   sticks plus 2 tablespoons
        margarine
1 1/2   cups flour
        pinch salt
3   teaspoons sugar
3/4   cup finely chopped pecans
1   8 ounce package
        cream cheese
2   cups powdered sugar
1   cup whipping cream,
        whipped
1   can cherry pie filling

Cut the first 4 ingredients together with pastry blender. Add pecans. Press in bottom of 13" x 9" pan or Pyrex dish. Bake 20 minutes in 350 degrees. Cool.

Cream together cream cheese and powdered sugar. Fold in whipped cream. Pour cherry pie filling on top. Refrigerate several hours or overnight. Chocolate pie filling can be used instead of cherry.

Wedding Anniversary Pie

"A CARAMEL APPLE BLISS"

Mary Louise and Bill Orr

Prepare topping first. For topping, put last 5 ingredients in a small saucepan and stir over low heat until melted. Now prepare crust. Preheat oven to 450 degrees. Using a standard 9 inch pie crust, prick the dough. Then lightly brush dough with the beaten white of an egg using a pastry brush. Put crust on a cookie sheet and bake for 3 minutes to let egg white set. Finally, prepare filling by mixing together dry ingredients in a small bowl. Peel and core apples (about 6 medium), and then slice thin. Mix the apples into the dry ingredients and add lemon juice and melted butter. Stir the mixture and immediately assemble pie. Place filling into cooled crust, and drizzle caramel topping all over filling. Place in preheated 450 degree oven and immediately reduce heat to 350 degrees. Bake at 350 degrees for 50 minutes or until apples are soft and cooked through. If crust appears to be getting too brown, lightly lay strips of aluminum foil over crust. Allow pie to cool completely before cutting. ❧

PREP TIME: 1 1/2 hours.
COOK TIME: 50 minutes.

It is important to slice the apples right before assembling and baking the pie. Otherwise, all the natural apple juice will be left in the mixing bowl! Brushing the crust with egg white and setting the egg white before assembly helps to keep the crust from getting soggy during baking.

Servings: 8

Pie:

1	pie crust (9 inch)
6	cups Granny Smith apples, thinly sliced
2	tablespoons lemon juice
2	tablespoons cornstarch
1	teaspoon cinnamon
2	tablespoons butter, melted
1/2	teaspoon salt

Topping:

1/4	teaspoon butter
1/2	teaspoon brown sugar, packed
2	tablespoons half and half
1/2	cup pecans, chopped
20	caramel candies

TESTED RECIPE

PER SERVING: 287 CALORIES: ❧ 14G FAT (42% CALORIES FROM FAT) ❧ 41G CARBOHYDRATE
3G PROTEIN ❧ 11MG CHOLESTEROL ❧ 360MG SODIUM

Thank You. *Very special thanks to my brother,*

Wilton E. Woods, for all his efforts on the narrative. Many thanks to my relatives and friends all around the country for their help and enthusiasm; to our three wonderful children, Wayne W., Virginia, and Charles; our daughter-in-law Mary Jane; our son-in-law Randy Shapiro; and our adored grandsons, William, John, and Benjamin Windle; and unending love and appreciation to my husband, Wayne E. Windle.

The parts of three actors were edited from the film to comply with time limitations. I am appreciative of their help — Morgana Shaw, Kirk Sisco, and Jonathan Brent.

> *Leann Phenix*
>
> *Nacho Garcia*
>
> *Bea Bragg*
>
> *Edith Firoozi Fried*
>
> *Anne Hebert*
>
> *Naomi Moore*
>
> *Dory Grace*
>
> *Kristen Tucker Pierce*
>
> *Lynne Henderlong-Rhea*
>
> *Bill Hanson*
>
> *Craig Anderson Productions*
>
> *The CBS Network*
>
> *The cast of the True Women Miniseries*

Chef Amy Chaisson Selig tested many of the featured dishes in the *True Women Cookbook*, adapting the antique recipes of Texas settlers for the contemporary kitchen. The Tested Recipes are noted.

With a Cajun father and an Italian mother, Amy was born with a passion for good food. Now residing in Houston, Texas, Amy puts her culinary experience to work through her business, *Your Personal Chef*. In addition to in-home culinary services, Amy gives cooking lessons and demonstrations, serves as a guest speaker on various culinary topics, and provides culinary consultation. The food she prepares for her clients complies with American Heart Association guidelines, and her repertoire includes Italian, French, Cajun, Creole, Fusion, and New American Cuisines.

Artist Anne Bell graces the pages of the *True Women Cookbook* with her original paintings of the book's historical heroines and the actresses portraying them in the CBS miniseries, *True Women*.

A prolific artist, Anne Bell is widely recognized not only for her rare ability to capture exact likenesses, but also for an uncanny talent for portraying the most winning aspects of the personality of her subjects. Based in Winter Springs, Florida, Anne Bell has won numerous awards, including regional, national, and local area juried shows, and she has been part of exhibits on national tours. A specialist in classic oil portraits, her numerous acclaimed works also include murals, bronze portraits, and bas-relief bronze plaques on display in public and private institutions across the country.

INDEX OF RECIPES

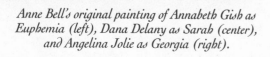

Anne Bell's original painting of Annabeth Gish as Euphemia (left), Dana Delany as Sarah (center), and Angelina Jolie as Georgia (right).

STEVE BOEHM

Janice Woods Windle is a lifelong Texan. She was born in San Antonio and grew up in the small town of Seguin, birthplace of her novel, *True Women*. The mother of three adult children, she lives in El Paso with her husband Wayne Windle, a prominent attorney.

Windle is employed as the President of the El Paso Community Foundation, an organization at the forefront of bi-national grantmaking. She became Chief Executive Officer in 1977 and since then, the foundation's assets have surged from $95,000 to nearly $55 million.

Windle is a graduate of the University of Texas at El Paso. In 1995, she was honored with a resolution from the Texas Senate for her achievements as an author and as a community fundraiser.

To order additional copies of
The True Women Cookbook,
please call 1-800-550-9659.

❦

To order copies of the novel
True Women in paperback,
please call 1-800-733-3000.

❦

To contact the author, or for
speaking information or media information, please contact:

Janice Woods Windle
c/o Phenix & Phenix Literary
Publicists, Inc.
1604 Nueces Street
Austin, Texas 78701
Phone: 512-478-2028
Fax: 512-478-2117

www.phenixpub.com
e-mail: lphenix@jumpnet.com

To schedule a *True Women* tour,
please contact:

Seguin Area Chamber of Commerce
427 N. Austin Street
Seguin, Texas 78155
Phone: 1-800-580-7322
Fax: 1-210-379-6971

McClure-Braches Properties
Committee
830 St. Paul Street
Gonzales, Texas 78629
Phone: 1-800-892-0214

To make a tax deductible donation
to preserve sites written about in
True Women, please contact:

Seguin Conservation Society
P.O. Box 245
Seguin, Texas 78156-0245
Phone: 210-379-1661

McClure-Braches Properties
Committee
830 St. Paul Street
Gonzales, Texas 78629
Phone: 1-800-892-0214